Gobbledy

Gobbledy

A Novel

By

Lis Anna-Langston

Published by SparkPress, a BookSparks imprint,
A division of SparkPoint Studio, LLC
Phoenix, Arizona, USA, 85007
www.gosparkpress.com

Published 2020
Printed in the United States of America
Print ISBN: 978-1-68463-067-7
E-ISBN: 978-1-68463-068-4
Library of Congress Control Number: 2020908692

Illustrations by Rich Powell
Book design by Stacey Aaronson

For Mark, *for everything*
& for Little A

One

Tiny dots of stars and planets form constellations above my head. Orion. The bear. The great hunter. I'm only eleven, but I know a lot about the stars. It's where my mom lives now. I come out on cool, clear evenings through the broken window in the attic to lie on the roof and listen for the sound of her voice.

"Dexter?" A voice whispers to the left of my head.

I look over. My little brother Dougal leans out of the window, looking first at me, then up into the sparkling sky. "Aren't you cold?"

I shrug, feeling the scratchy shingles beneath my jacket. "I like it out here."

Dougal swings a leg through the window. Where I'm lying is the flattest part of the roof. On either side it swoops up so steep that even I won't climb it. Dougal stops in the windowsill, letting his legs dangle. His big personality makes it easy for me to forget that he's only eight years old. Eight and a half, he'll point out. Still, even for someone almost nine, he looks tiny in the window with the glow of light from the attic.

When Mom was here, she spent hours in the attic, building a small replica of the town where we live. She didn't grow up here. She said she picked this small town in Pennsylvania because, to her, it was the most magical place on Earth. Mom had answers for everything. Maybe that's why I spend so much time on the roof, hoping to see a sign that she's listening.

The Cricket Colony had been Mom's idea. Since me and my best friend, Fiona, spend so much time in the forest near our house, she'd suggested I make adventure a part of my grade. Tomorrow I turn in the crickets for my end-of-the-semester science project. Then I have to turn them loose back in the forest, where they'll make homes under thick beds of leaves to stay warm. But I'll miss them a lot.

Dougal shivers. "Dad was weird tonight."

I nod. "Dad's been weird every night for a few months now."

Stars sparkle in the dark sky. We all want her back, even if we don't talk about it. Instead, we talk about far-off galaxies.

My little brother points to the sky. "There's Andromeda."

It was Mom's favorite, because you can see it just by lying on a roof at the end of autumn. Mom said things like, "I believe that's a globular cluster," and "Stars are old." She said that when stars die, they sometimes leave a black hole behind to remind everyone they were alive once. There is definitely a hole in our family. Not a bad hole, but a big hole. The kind of hole that sneaks up on me late at night when I remember. So, sometimes, I climb out here to forget.

My walkie-talkie crackles to life on the flat space next to me. "Gamma Ray to Cosmic. Come in, Cosmic."

Dougal leans forward, trying to get a look at the Little Dipper.

I press the button. "Cosmic here."

"Whew. I thought you'd slipped into another dimension."

"Hardly. I'm up on the roof."

Fi is quiet a second; then she says, "Any signs yet?"

"Nope. But sometimes these things take a while."

"Speaking of taking a while, I gotta wake up super early to finish my project, so I gotta get some sleep."

"Got a title yet?"

She laughs. "Nope." A second passes. "Tell Dougal I said goodnight, and I'll be out back in the morning."

Dougal softly yells, "Goodnight," over my shoulder and pushes off to go inside.

Someday I want to be able to sleep under the stars without having to worry about rolling off the roof. Mom said space is full of magic, but there isn't much magic since she left. I guess that's just how it is sometimes. I stand up, stretching.

I'm ready for adventure. Except it's late, and Dad hates it when I wake him up, going up and down the stairs.

I climb back through the window and look at the

attic. An old sofa with a stack of books on building miniatures; a work table with the village on top; Mom's favorite blanket; a cart full of brushes, glue, and a few big jars like the one I used to make my Cricket Colony.

Out of the corner of my eye, I see a flash and turn. There, blazing its way across the dark, is the most incredible falling star I've ever seen. It's so close, I swear I can hear the sizzle. I know it's a sign. I squeeze my eyes shut and make a wish.

Two

Wooden boards rattle under our feet as we run across the bridge leading into the forest.

My lungs burn trying to catch up. "What are we doing?"

Fi is so far ahead she has to yell, glancing back over her shoulder, "Remember those cameras I set up for my science project?"

"Yeah?" I heave, about to collapse.

"Well, you're gonna want to see this," she says, before making an abrupt turn into my favorite cluster of pine trees.

I hear her purple cowboy boots pounding the dirt but can't see her anymore. I slow to a stop, bending over to catch my breath. My watch says it's been exactly eight and a half minutes since Fiona burst through my back door and interrupted my bowl of cereal. I look around.

"*Dexter!*" Fi yells, loud and clear, up ahead.

I roll my eyes, push myself upright, and try to run. It's more like stumbling, but it works. I run past the fallen oak, under the low-hanging limbs of a maple, around the corner into the clearing, and slow to a stop.

It's the place we always come. Fi pulls her backpack off, pointing to the ground a few feet away. Tiny, cream-colored mushrooms sparkle in the dim morning sun. Light floats up, like fizz on soda. The mushrooms grow in circles, but as I kneel down, I see they aren't really mushrooms. They are like really strange, tiny trees. Inside one of the circles is a flat, golden rock.

"Whoa," I say, leaning closer. "What are these?"

Fi shakes her head. "I have no idea."

"Did you look these things up? I've never seen anything like this out here before."

"I didn't have time. I got up early to finish my project and saw this on the footage. Then I ran next door to your house."

I crouch down, touching the ground.

"You know how we set the sensors to send me a notification if the cameras turned on? Well, they turned on in the middle of the night. I got the email when I woke up. Just in case there was some last-minute thing I could add to my project today, I ran through the footage. It was like the cameras burst into flames, and then it went all staticky, and when the picture came back on, I saw these mushrooms." Fi frowns. "But only a few of my cameras were still working."

"Wait a minute. You're telling me these things grew in a few minutes?"

Fi fills her cheeks with air and raises an eyebrow like she does when she really doesn't believe the facts. "It appears so."

I reach out to touch a mushroom thingy and it shocks me. I pull my finger back immediately. A tiny, red dot swells on the tip.

"What's wrong?"

"It shocked me!"

Fi scrunches up her nose, "*What?*" She hovers over them like a buzzard. "It shocked you? How? There's no such thing as electric mushrooms." Carefully she reaches down to touch the top of a mushroom and pulls her hand back. "Ouch!" Fi looks at me and then the mushroom. "I hope that's not poisonous."

We exchange a look. Electric, glittery, mushroom *thingies.* Suddenly, my cereal getting soggy is not my top priority. Fi stands and walks to a small camera rigged to a tree trunk. Even from a distance, I can tell it's smoked.

Fi crouches down next to the camera, and I watch. She's wearing her favorite purple cowboy boots and her cat-ear headband. She's been my best friend since second grade, when her family moved in next to mine, and her cat, Sir Shreds-A-Lot, dug up Mom's flower bed. Some kids in my class think it's weird that a girl is my best friend, but anyone who knows Fi knows that isn't weird at all. She's pretty much the coolest kid in fifth grade. Her dad has all kinds of crazy camera stuff in their house, and he lets her use it, which is beyond awesome, since my dad says I'm not responsible enough to own a hamster, much less a camera. Fi and I have been recording chipmunks and squirrels gathering nuts for weeks now for her project. Which is due. In about forty-five minutes.

"Dexter?"

I jerk my head up and see Fi standing with her hands on her hips. "I'm going down to the river. Something happened out here for sure."

As soon as she rounds the path down to the river, I reach for the golden rock. I have to be careful not to touch any mushrooms. I shock myself twice before I get a firm grip on the shimmering, golden rock. I'm collecting clues.

Fiona pops her head around a tree and points to a charred path of dirt. "I heard a noise last night. I thought I was dreaming."

I inspect the burnt tree logs and shimmering mushroom thingies as I slip the rock in my pocket, hoping it doesn't shock me. "I did, too."

Fi digs around in her backpack and pulls out a small camera. The kind you see in spy movies.

"Isn't your dad going to miss all this stuff?"

"It's old surveillance stuff from an embassy he worked at. He just shoves it all in the basement. Daddy is a pack rat."

I've never been to an embassy.

Neither has anyone in my family.

In my family, we're still arguing over who takes out the trash, which is usually me, since I can't stop getting in trouble.

"Listen," I say, "I can't be late. My dad is still mad

about the tooth thing. I've got to get home and get my crickets to turn in today."

Fi slings her backpack over her shoulder, "If we run, we have plenty of time to make first bell. I'll set up my laptop in the computer lounge and see what these mushrooms do when no one's looking."

Three

I am right in the middle of a pop quiz when I glance down and see an army of crickets pouring out of my backpack. I swoop down to grab the four hopping closest to my tennis shoes. They shoot straight up in the air and scatter in all directions. In horrifyingly slow motion—which is not something crickets are usually known for—I watch a big one bend its back legs for a split second before launching into the air. It lands on Sally Summer's knee sock, clinging sideways. A second cricket lands on her knee, most likely to keep the first company.

This is how disaster forms.

Sally rockets out of her seat, half falling, half stumbling into the desk of our teacher, who isn't there because she stepped out.

Sally runs in circles, swatting desperately at her legs. Her brown bob swirls around her head like a tornado.

Crickets hop frantically about, looking for a place to hide. Crickets are friendly, kind little bugs who live in happy communities. Crickets are related to the grass-hopper and the katydid. They have excellent vision. There are nine hundred species of cricket world-wide. None of my classmates appreciate these facts.

I know all this thanks to the field guide I've been compiling for weeks, which has been knocked to the floor in the hullabaloo. Bobby Roberts snatches it up to smash a cricket.

"*What* are you doing!" I scream. "That's a life form *and* my grade you're about to kill."

Half my classmates are balanced on top of their desks. The other half—presumably the half not bothered by insects—stand around the room, mouths open, gawking. Trouble is a plague. Trouble follows fun. Trouble is my mortal enemy.

I grab my backpack and see clearly for the first time that the lid to the Cricket Colony was screwed on crooked. Since I was in a massive hurry to get the crickets out of the house this morning, I must have knocked it loose. This counts for a third of my grade. Panic seizes me. I pull the lid off completely to make sure no crickets get smooshed. In the bottom of the jar, with only two crickets left, is the strangest bug I've ever seen.

Quickly, I stuff the jar deep into my backpack and make a run for the door.

Fi is standing in the hallway. "Why is Sally screaming?"

I glance down at the bathroom pass in her hand. "Umm . . . something is weird."

She furrows her brow. "Weird how?"

I push open the nearest door and wave for her to follow.

I unzip the top of my backpack and slowly pull the Cricket Colony jar out. Fi hunches over and stares at the strange little bug standing next to the crickets. "What is that?"

The little bug screeches loudly.

I shrug. "I don't know. It must have been stuck to that rock I picked up this morning in the forest. I really, really need a good grade, so I put the rock inside the colony to brighten it up."

Fi looks inside the jar, then back at me. "Where's the rock?"

"I think it got knocked under the dirt."

The strange little bug looks up at me with a wild look in its eyes.

Fi's mouth drops open, "*Oh, my god.* What *is* that thing?"

I shrug, feeling my shoulders slump forward. "I don't know, exactly. What I do know is that it took us weeks to catch all those crickets."

Fi thinks about this a second. "Okay, listen. You go back to class and round up those crickets before your teacher gets back. I'll meet you in the computer lounge after the bell, and we'll try and figure out what's going on."

I nod and walk straight into the hall, where Principal Snarly Watson stops to look at me. We lock eyes. Her crooked tooth shines in the hall light. After a second, I try to walk around her, but she blocks me. She points to the door behind me. Annoyed, I turn around and see

GIRLS RESTROOM printed in big letters across the door. Suddenly, I know crickets are no longer at the top of my list of things to worry about.

🎁

In the main part of the office, a printer rumbles. Snarly walks into her office, clutching copies of my disciplinary action. She walks behind her desk and sits down. I stare at my shoes, the ones Mom bought me, with flames painted down the sides to help me run faster.

"Why can't you be funny and smart like your little brother, Dougal?"

"Because then I wouldn't be myself."

She snorts, baring her crooked tooth. "Given the circumstances, that wouldn't be such a bad thing." Leaning back in her chair, she says, "This is worse than selling your little brother's tooth."

Two lone crickets chirp in the jar. The little bug is nowhere to be seen.

"It's not like he needed it anymore," I point out.

Her nose twitches. "Do you want to tell me what you were doing in the girls' bathroom?"

"My crickets—"

"I heard that part already. Here's the issue: Crickets escaping in no way explains why you were in the girls' bathroom."

I cannot get Fi in trouble. I just cannot. I hesitate, think hard, then finally say, "I was going to get a trashcan to trap the crickets. It's my grade. I was desperate."

She stares straight at me. "There's a trashcan in the classroom."

Seconds pass. The crickets chirp again. I sit silent, unable to think of a good reason to be in the girls' bathroom.

"So. . . ." She exhales. "Then explain why you let the bugs loose."

"I didn't let them loose. They're my science project."

"This is worse than the toilet incident," Snarly pinches her face up, recoiling in horror at the memory.

I roll my eyes and lean back. *That was a science experiment.*

Snarly spins around in her chair and grabs a stack of papers. She flips through them quickly, pulls one out, and hands it over to me. "I am putting you in the Drama Club."

I stare at the call for members. "My punishment is being forced to join a club?"

"Not just any club. This club has the annual Winter Extravaganza coming up. That should give you something to do other than hang around my office."

"*What?* You can't do this."

She stands up from her desk, ignoring me. "I hear they need a Gingerbread Man."

"I don't want to join the Drama Club."

"Then you shouldn't start so much drama."

The main door to the office slams shut, and I turn. Dad walks in, wearing his work jacket and a tight frown. Not a good combination. I shove the piece of paper into my backpack.

"Oh, good, Mr. Duckworth, you're here." Snarly pulls a fake smile that showcases her crooked tooth.

Dad doesn't even pretend to be nice. "I was informed that Dexter is in some kind of trouble."

She clears her throat. "Well, yes. Trouble seems to follow him around. His bug farm filled a classroom with creepy-crawlies, and then I caught him hiding in the girls' bathroom."

Dad furrows his brow, "Is he suspended?"

With a huff, she whips the disciplinary action around and slaps it on the counter. "We can all hope for that one day. Until then, he goes home early."

My eyes shoot to the jar, scoping it out for the little bug thing. Two crickets sit on top of the dirt. Either the bug escaped in the classroom, or he's buried himself in the dirt. Either way, as long as I don't get in too much trouble, going home early is perfectly fine. The urgency to get out of the principal's office collides with a gut-wrenching reality: The school has called my father at the ketchup factory three times this month.

Snarly points at the dotted line. "Sign here, and he can be your problem for the rest of the day."

Dad wrestles with a pen chained to the counter. "Thanks, but I'm pretty sure he's my problem for life."

Four

In the parking lot, Dad jams his key into his old station wagon, jiggling the lock. The car is so old it's practically glued together, but Dad refuses to give it up because he took Mom on her first date in the ugly contraption.

I stuff the jar into my backpack, careful not to jostle the survivors. From this, I can rebuild.

Still jiggling his key in the lock, because he is alternately too cheap or too busy to get it fixed (his words, not mine), he asks, "And while we're on the subject of doing bad things, I'd like to know what in the world made you sell your brother's teeth?'

We've already been over that. "Tooth," I correct.

"Tooth, then."

"Because he didn't need it anymore."

"That doesn't mean you can *sell* it."

"Well, it's not like he's going to jam it back in his mouth and use it."

Imaginary missiles shoot from his eyes. "Those decorative jars belonged to your mother. And you've filled them with bugs. God knows what you've done that I haven't found about out yet." Dad slumps over the roof of his station wagon.

I look up and down the boulevard, where silver Christmas stars twinkle from the tops of telephone poles. I am quiet. I focus on the dry, gray trees that look like stick figures against the sky. December winds have blown the autumn colors away. When Dougal was little, he couldn't say Christmas, so he called it Kissmas. Since Mom had never been very religious, we started calling it by the new name. This will be the first Kissmas without her. It's depressing.

Dad's hands drop to his sides. He looks up into the sky and takes a long, deep *relaxation breath* just like on the CD he listens to at night. Exhale to a count of ten, nine, eight, seven . . .

He stops abruptly and drops his eyes to meet mine. "You're on Red. If you stay on Red, or, God forbid, go *Code* Red, then you're not going to your grandparents' house."

Ugh. The knot in my stomach twists tighter.

"If I keep having to leave work and pick you up, I'm not driving you all the way to meet your grandparents this year. There will also be no TV, no games, no computer, no Fiona. Just you and the four walls of your bedroom. Got it? No more trouble. No more ridiculous antics."

"Got it. No more trouble." I cross my heart.

He rolls his eyes, unconvinced. "And no more bugs. Stop dragging every single critter you find into our house. Just stop. I mean, really. Tadpoles in the bathtub. That feral cat colony you tried to start in the backyard. The chicken in the closet. It's all too much! Understand? It's just me now, and I can't keep dealing with all the drama you cook up."

I nod. Dry leaves tumble down the sidewalk.

The station wagon door groans open. "Build a volcano or something. No, wait . . . don't build a volcano. Just do something that doesn't end with me picking you up from the principal's office."

"All I want is a pet," I say.

"And all I want is for you to stop getting in trouble."

I frown.

"Do we understand each other?"

I huff. "Yes, I understand."

For a split second, Dad looks at me over the roof of the ugly station wagon, and I think he's going to say something nice, but he pinches his frown tighter and climbs inside.

At home, I pull open the door to a tiny room under the stairs and set the cricket jar on my main work table. This is the lab where I do all my research. So far, it's been one long experiment in trouble. One side has shelves filled with supplies and logs. The other side has a ceiling that slants over my table. The darkest corner of the table, wedged against the wall, contains my most important, most involved experiments. That's where the Cricket Colony formed. Now I don't know what I'm going to do.

I pull the string above my head. The light bulb flickers and sputters out.

Dad rounds the corner and nearly has a heart attack. "What on Earth are you doing?" he asks.

"I have to check on an experiment."

Dad frowns, thrusting his hand out. "Stop being weird and hand the jars over." He leans down, staring into my lab. "All of them."

"I— have to transfer a few experiments."

Laying his hand on the doorframe, he taps his finger loudly. "I'll wait. And while I am waiting, you can tell me why you ever thought using your mother's decorative jars for dirt was a good idea."

I unscrew the lid. The little crickets look up at me. "Because I was forbidden to take jars and bowls from the kitchen."

"So, you thought taking antique jars that belonged to your mom was a better idea?"

I don't know what I was thinking now. I catch the crickets in one hand and hold them gently as I dump the dirt into a smaller, dark brown jar. I can't find the other bug, but the golden rock is buried in the dirt.

Dad clears his throat, "I have ketchup to attend to, Son. I don't have time for this."

I dump the dirt quickly into the jar and turn around. I slide my hand into the new jar and watch the crickets jump onto the dirt. I take a lid I poked holes into and screw it on extra tight.

He points under my experiment table.

"There's another one."

I half smile and pull it out.

Dad grumbles off down the hall.

Five seconds later, the back door opens, and Fi yells, "Dex-man!"

I stick my head out of my lab and yell back, "In my lab."

She catches up to me in the hall, swinging her laptop.

Dad stops in the kitchen doorway. "Hello, Fiona. Dexter is in big trouble. I don't think he can have company right now."

Fi looks at me out of the corner of her eye. "My sister Fran is at home and would be happy to look after Dex and me, if you have to go back to work."

Here's the thing: Ketchup, like me, cannot be left unattended. I can see the work wheels turning in Dad's head. He doesn't want to admit it, but he has to go. Without saying a word, he walks over to my behavior chart in the kitchen and slides the arrow in-between Red and Code Red.

Queue the doom music. The only thing beyond Code Red is being grounded for life.

He turns, patiently staring at Fi. "Are you sure this is all right with your sister?"

"Yes, Mr. D., you can text her if you want."

Dad looks at both of us a second longer and jingles the keys in his pocket. "I'll be home later."

Dad's ringtone for work is "The Imperial March"

from *Star Wars*. It starts up in his pocket. *Dun dun dun da dun dun da dun dun.* Dad sighs and walks out the back door. "They're probably calling to fire me for leaving work constantly."

Ouch.

I wait until he's gone, then lean in to Fi, "What are you doing here?"

"I saw you leaving with your dad and called my sister to pick me up."

"And she did?"

"Of course, she did. I told her I have a stomachache. Listen, I got footage of what those mushroom-shaped things do when no one is looking. Something weird is going on in the forest. I want you to see this. Those weird mushroom things glow and look like they're breathing. Where's the bug?"

I shrug. "I don't know. He wasn't in the jar."

She squishes up her nose. "Okay. Do you know where it went?"

I sigh, big and loud. "I had a lot going on, what with my dad and the principal."

Setting the laptop on the hall table, she flips the screen up and presses a few keys. Night vision scenes of the forest fill the screen. At first, not much happens. Then static, a bleep, more static, and streaks of light fill the screen. "This was last night."

I look at Fi. Fi looks at me. She presses a key on the laptop. "This is today." On screen, a fuzzy image of the mushroom thingies comes into view. Fi presses the arrow key and the camera moves. The mushroom thingies move too. They all turn, like they are looking at the camera. Little lightning bolts shoot from their tips.

"Whoa," I say. "Are those things alive?"

Fi shrugs. "Maybe. But I think they're some kind of electrical device."

I lean in closer to the screen. "Why?"

She nudges me like I'm a total dork. "Because of the electrical charge."

"Oh, right."

The mushroom thingies turn away from the camera and fold up, like flower petals.

"What do you think these things are?" she asks.

A loud wail comes from the new jar full of dirt.

Five

Slowly, I lift the jar off the work table and unscrew the lid. Fi and I look down at the strange bug. The little thing wails. It's not much bigger than the two crickets standing on the sidelines, staring.

Fi looks at me with a wild look in her eyes. "Does your dad know?"

I shake my head. "Absolutely not. No. Dad will just make me take him back to the forest."

I pull the lid off. The strange little bug opens his mouth really big.

"Okay, okay," I whisper. "I'll feed you, but you have to be quiet."

He closes his mouth and blinks. For a second, I think he might actually understand what I'm saying.

There's a bag of potato chips on the counter in the kitchen. I drop chips into the jar one by one, avoiding the crickets.

Chomp. Chomp. Chomp.

"Where's the rock?" Fi asks.

Chomp. Chomp. Chomp.

The back door opens. Startled, Fi jerks upright

abruptly, smacking her head on the slanted ceiling. I try to grab her hand as it flies past my face. Her arms flap wildly as she falls in a woozy, slow motion out into the hall.

"Fi?" I say loudly.

Ka-thunk.

"*Fi?*" I drop to the floor next to her and check her pulse, like I've seen people do in movies. "Can you hear me?"

She undoubtedly cannot. She does not move or answer.

The jar wobbles on the wooden table.

"Excuse me," I quickly step over her limp body and grab the jar. I tighten my grip as it jerks around in my arms. Herky-jerky, it shifts against my shirt. I hold tight and screw the lid back on.

"Dexter?"

Huh? "What are you doing home, Dougal?" I yell.

"I live here."

"I know that, but you're early."

"Not really. School is out. Dad asked Fran to pick me up because you got in trouble again, and he couldn't leave work twice."

"Umm . . ."

Fran walks into the hall and says, "Oh my gosh, what happened?"

I look left, then right. Up, then down. Over, then under. My eyes settle on my backpack next to my work table. I shove the jar inside quickly, listening to the herky-jerky sound of glass tapping against my note-books. I cover the jar with my jacket and step quickly into the hall.

Fran pulls her hand to her mouth. "What happened to Fi?"

Fi is on the floor where I left her.

"She was, *umm,* we were doing our science projects, and then she fainted."

"I thought you had to turn those in today?"

"We did, but mine got loose and she was . . ."

I stare at her limp, oddly twisted body.

"Do you want me to perform CPR until the emergency workers arrive?" Dougal asks.

Fran rolls Fiona over on her back. "There'll be no emergency workers. I got this," she says quietly, tapping Fi's cheeks. "Fiona?"

Fi's eyes pop open. "*Wha?*"

"You passed out, girl. Are you okay?"

"*Huh?*"

Fran helps Fi to her feet. She sways, woozy, reaching for the wall.

Their cat, Sir Shreds-A-Lot, scratches and howls at the back door.

"Don't let that cat in," Dougal says. "He's been sneaking up to the attic and eating the villagers in Mom's village."

"What's the last thing you remember?" I ask Fi.

She rubs her forehead. "Let me get an ice pack. I'll answer that in a minute."

Six

From my bedroom window, I watch Fran walk Fi across the driveway. Cool, gray light fans out across the dark outline of branches, highlighting the occasional dry leaf still hanging on. Bats screech on their way down to the boulevard. On the other side of the glass, silvery light glints off an abandoned spider web. As soon as they turn the corner, I go for the jar.

Dougal stands in the doorway, giving me the silent-but-deadly stare. "What are you doing?"

It takes a second to manufacture a convincing lie. "Looking at a spider web."

Dougal studies me, his brow pinched tight. He's two years younger than me but mature in dog years. He clears his throat and announces, "We've got a family meeting tonight."

I step away from the window.

Clunk clunk.

Starting with the closet, Dougal's eyes trail around the room, stopping on my backpack. "What's that noise?"

I'm about to say I don't hear anything when—

Clunk clunk clunk.

He points. "It's in your backpack."

"It's a pack of Mexican jumping beans I bought to-day."

Dougal tilts his head sideways like he always does when he doesn't believe me. "Can I see them?"

"I thought you wanted to talk about the meeting," I blurt out.

He patiently lays his hand on the dresser and taps with his index finger. "Mexican jumping beans first."

Clank clank clunk.

My eyes jerk to the backpack.

Clank clank clunk.

The sound is louder, more insistent.

Clunk clunk clunk.

I walk over to my closet and pretend to look for something. *Anything.*

Dougal clears his throat.

I ignore him.

More throat clearing.

I have a pretty good idea how stubborn he can be. More than that, I'm worried he'll tell Dad. I can't afford any more trouble. Whatever is in that jar could send me into Code Red.

"What?" I hiss, glancing back over my shoulder.

He points. "You're stalling. I'm giving you one chance to tell me what you're hiding."

"Or what?"

"Or I'm calling the Humane Society and telling them you're endangering the lives of Mexican jumping beans by keeping them trapped in a backpack."

"They're not trapped."

"Prove it."

I huff. "Why won't you drop the beans?"

"Because I know you. Anything worth hiding is worth seeing."

Okay. He's got me there.

Clunk clunk clunk.

Dougal looks back at me. "If you haven't unzipped that backpack in ten seconds then I'm doing it. One. Two."

"Okay. Okay." I stomp over.

He stops counting and stares at me instead.

I can do this. I place my hand on the zipper and jerk it to the side. The jar is exactly where I left it. Air holes poked in the top look like prehistoric code. Lamplight glimmers off the metal.

Clunk clunk clunk.

Dougal reaches down, but I snatch it up quickly.

I pause, listening. "Close the door and lock it," I whisper.

My normally uncooperative little brother runs over, closes the door without a sound, and flips the lock. My eyes squeeze shut for a second. I carefully set the jar on the floor. It wobbles. Dougal walks over and kneels down. I sit down on the floor and unscrew the lid. Sucking in a huge breath, I lean over and look inside. Two glowing eyes stare back at me. Dougal gasps and falls backwards on his heels. The glowing eyes are attached to a small, furry body that's grown to the size of a quarter. A strange little bug. The little furry thing opens his mouth and shrieks. I put the lid back on. A low wail emerges from the jar.

"What is that thing?" Dougal whispers.

I shrug. "I don't know exactly, but he's getting bigger. I picked up a rock in the forest. I think he must have been stuck to it, and I didn't notice."

"That's definitely not a bug," he says, matter-of-factly. "I spent all last summer studying insects, and that's not one of them."

"He has to be a bug," I insist.

The thing wails again.

I look down into the jar, suddenly realizing it's empty. "He *ate* my crickets! My last two crickets."

Dougal crinkles his nose, "Eww."

Everything inside the jar is gone, including the dirt. The bug opens his mouth wide and yowls.

"I think it's hungry," Dougal observes.

"He ate my *grade*."

Dougal stands upright. "When did you last feed it?"

I furrow my brow, a little annoyed by the question. "Well, I haven't really fed him. I gave him a few potato chips, though."

He looks me directly in the eye. "You've been holding it captive and you didn't even *feed* it?"

"I didn't *know* he was living in here. This is supposed to be a cricket habitat. Thank you very much."

Dougal runs quietly down the stairs. His absence gives me a minute to think. What did I put in the jar? Dirt. Crickets. *The golden rock. . . .*

Minutes later, Dougal returns with an armload of food.

It's my turn to raise an eyebrow. "That's a lot of food. This thing isn't very big."

Dougal plops down on the floor. "We don't know if it's an herbivore, insectivore, or carnivore. I grabbed a variety of food choices."

Okay. Good call. Maybe that's why Dougal is doing all the advanced projects, even though he's only in third grade. He pulls a hot dog out of his jacket pocket, bites off half, and lowers the other half down into the jar. "These are my favorite hot dogs. If he doesn't like them, we'll move onto parsley flakes and granola." The little thing wails again. Dougal drops the food into the jar, careful not to squash him.

There is a possibility, however small, that bugs might eat hot dogs.

"If I was a bug, I'd eat pizza," I say.

Gobble gobble gobble. Snarf snarf snarf.

Dougal and I look over the rim of the jar at the same time. The hot dog is gone. Dougal's eyes open wide. He shifts around, trying to see if the food rolled behind the bug. Finally, he looks me in the eye and says, "I think it just ate the whole thing."

Peering over the edge of the jar, I confirm that yes,

the hot dog is, in fact, gone. Two eyes blink. Then he opens his mouth.

"He's so small." I calculate the hot dog to be at least four times his size.

"It must be really hungry," Dougal observes, dropping chunks of granola down the sides.

Gobble gobble gobble.

Dougal drops a piece of yogurt-coated breakfast bar into the jar.

Snarf snarf snarf.

We peer over the edge. The little thing looks larger, almost the size of a half dollar.

Shaking his head, Dougal points down at the grumbling, big-eyed thing. "If it keeps eating like this, it's going to get bigger."

"Don't say that."

Dougal drops an organic cookie down the side.

Gobble gobble gobble.

"Are you sure you didn't put anything else in here?" His eyes narrow at the corners.

I honestly can't remember. The dirt I originally put in the jar could have contained any number of unexamined life forms. Then there's the golden rock, but rocks don't generally grow.

"Okay, we'll go to the forest, and you can show me where you got the stuff you put in the jar. We might be able to take it back."

It.

We don't even know what *it* is. Truthfully, sleeping

in the same room with *it* is going to be a little creepy. Dougal grabs the cap out of my hand and starts to screw it on tight. *It* wails. But I like *it*.

Dougal pauses, sighing. "I bet it needs some water, or something to sleep on."

I jump up, suddenly feeling dumb. This is my experiment. I don't need my little brother bossing me around.

"Where are you going?" Dougal whispers loudly.

"To the bathroom. Keep watch."

Back in the bedroom, I pull out a handful of cotton balls and drop them, one by one, into the jar. The strange little bug snatches them up quickly, stuffing them against the side of the jar with a grunt.

Dougal shakes his head. "What are you going to do with that thing?"

I look down. The little creature lies down on top of the cotton balls, feet straight in the air. His furry little chest rises and falls with each contented breath.

"He's trying to sleep," I whisper.

Dougal peers over the rim and frowns. "I can't believe you. Dad is going to freak out when he finds you harboring gobbledy little things."

"Hey, that's a good name. Gobbledy."

Dougal slaps his palm to his forehead. "You can't name it. If you name it, then you'll want to keep it."

"I already want to keep him."

My little brother jams his hands in his pocket just like Dad and glares at me.

I wrap the jar carefully in a warm jacket and put him

in my sock drawer to snooze. "We'll get Fi and go to the forest and see if we can pick up any clues. "

Dougal stands up, dusting off his hands. "And then what?"

I shrug. "And then I will figure out what to do with him."

"Uh-huh."

"It's not like I knew this was going to happen."

Dougal rolls his eyes and walks out of the room. "Famous last words," he says from the hall. "This is just like the time you found that chicken on the baseball field and tried to keep it in the closet."

"Boys," Dad yells up the stairs, "It's time for the meeting."

Seven

Dad's on the phone. I try to walk in without drawing attention, but he looks up and waves me over to a seat.

"Am I in trouble?" I ask.

Dad hangs up the phone. "Did you do something to get into trouble?"

I look at Dougal. He shrugs. Family meetings and waiting in line are his least favorite things.

"Not within the last few minutes," I offer.

Dad looks down at his work laptop and makes notes. Flecks of dried ketchup dot the sleeves of his jacket. He inhales long and jams his hands down into his pockets.

I look up and fake a smile.

Dad frowns. "Well, I guess the best way to say this is to just blurt it out, so here goes: we won't be going to the beach for Kissmas this year as a family."

Dougal raises his eyebrows but looks away.

My grandparents, G-mama and G-daddy, live in the coolest place on Earth: on a strip of sand down off the coast of Georgia. Dougal and I go three times a year.

Winter break, spring break, and summer vacation. It's like a holiday in paradise. It's the one thing our family always does together. Before we lost a family member. The one who handed out kisses on Kissmas morning. Real kisses on the cheeks, and little Hershey's Kisses while opening presents. Everything in our holiday house was Kissmas. Kissing reindeer. Kissing Mr. and Mrs. Claus. Kissing snow people and silly little puckered elves. It's all in the basement now, and not a single one of us wants to bring it upstairs.

Dad clears his throat, "I know this is kinda a bummer for you two, but I'm working overtime, worried about my job. We launched this new Special Limited-Edition Holiday Ketchup that's green and red in the bottle, but squeezes out brown, and is about to make me lose my mind. If you can stop getting in trouble, I will drive and meet your grandparents halfway, and you can go. But I have to stay here to solve this ketchup mystery." Dad looks straight at me, "And I will only do this if there is zero trouble from you, Dexter. I've got a lot of pressure on me right now. I don't need the added pressure of your shenanigans. I've got brown ketchup that looks like poo, Son. I can't be picking you up from school every day. It's just me now, and you're making this really hard."

All I want for Kissmas is sand, surf, eating out on the pier, buried treasure, and the biggest adventure I can find. And a dog. I want a dog.

"Okay," I say. "I understand."

"Meeting adjourned," Dad says.

Dougal stands and practically runs for the door.

Dad clears his throat, "Dexter?"

I am right behind Dougal but stop. I turn.

Dad holds out a small, brown cardboard box that says: HANDLE WITH CARE. PET ROCK. "Since I am not likely to lift the ban on a pet anytime soon, I got this for you. You can start with learning to take care of a Pet Rock."

Dad's pretty strange. Even before Mom died, he was marching to the beat of his own drum. I have no idea what to make of this gift, so I take it and say, "Okay. Thanks."

I am about to make a run for the stairs when there's a knock on the back door. I open it to find Fi, holding an ice pack on her head. Leaves skitter across the back porch no one has swept. Mom loved sweeping autumn leaves away. Loved whisking them up in the air with her broom. Now they sit, brown and clumped at the edges.

"How's your head?" I ask.

"Full of intrigue," she says, walking into the kitchen. "Where did you hide him?"

"Be quiet. My dad will hear you."

Dougal clears his throat behind us. "Dad's already back on the phone."

Eight

I am halfway up the stairs when I hear the first yowl. Once I am inside my bedroom, I slide to a stop in front of my dresser, unscrew the lid to the jar, and set it next to my Pet Rock. Gobbledy's face fills the opening. He's grown so much, he completely fills up the jar. He sucks in a long breath and stretches his furry arms up. I hold the jar up, searching frantically. Except for Gobbledy's fur pressing against the glass, I can't see anything. I hold the jar over my head to look at the bottom.

Gobbledy huffs deep, long breaths.

I wrap my arms around the jar and run for the stairs leading to the attic.

Dougal and Fi stare at encyclopedias in the upstairs hall, running their fingers along the spines.

I whisper quick, urgent. "Meet me in the attic. Pronto. We've got a situation."

Dougal snorts, "He pooped in your drawer, didn't he?"

I run full-throttle up the stairs, dodge the table where Mom was building a miniature village, and run straight for the old fold-out sofa bed. I spin around and hold the jar up for Dougal and Fi to see. Gobbledy's small, furry face sticks out of the top of the jar.

"Whoa," Dougal drops an encyclopedia. "What happened? He was tiny when we went downstairs."

A knock on the attic door gets our attention. Dad yells up the stairs, "Hey, is anybody up there?"

My entire body freezes.

"Umm . . . yes," Dougal answers.

"What are you doing?"

Gobbledy yowls.

Everyone is silent for a moment, then Dad says, "Huh, that was weird. I wanted to tell you that dinner will be ready later than usual. If you need a snack, then come on down. And be careful up there. Your mom put a lot of work into that village. Don't touch anything up here, especially her telescope."

"Okay," Dougal says. "I'll make sure no one touches anything."

"I will leave you in charge." Dad closes the door at the bottom of the stairs. Which doesn't really close, because the latch is broken, so it just bangs against the frame.

Dougal wags a finger at the small, furry thing filling up the jar. "You can't make so much noise."

Gobbledy yowls again.

"I'm going to get food," I say.

"I'll go with you," Fi says.

"No way." Dougal drops his arms to his sides, backing up. "I will not be left alone with that thing. I'll get the snacks. You two wait up here and keep that wild beast quiet." At the top of the stairs, he turns. "We need to figure out what he is, so we can figure out what to do with him."

My little brother stomps down to the second floor.

I point my finger at the furry creature. "You are in trouble, mister. *You* ate the survivors of my science project."

Gobbledy squeals and points back at me. I want to strangle him.

"He's definitely not an insect." Fi tilts her head, "He looks like a cross between a prairie dog, a chinchilla, and a cartoon."

I can see it. Big ears, with tufts of fur that droop from the tips, and these long skinny arms and legs. A perfectly round body covered in soft, gray fur. *If,* and only *if,* he stops growing. I glance around the attic, "I need somewhere to hide him."

Outside, an autumn wind plows its way through the trees. The broken window in the attic flaps against the frame. Little flecks of paint, worn loose in a scattered frenzy, dust the hardwood floor. *Rat-a-tat-tat,* the window thumps. It's been broken since last spring. Everything broke last spring.

I lay the jar on the sofa bed and hold tight. Gobbledy squeezes and grunts until his furry body slides through the opening.

Fascinated by the village, he runs over to inspect it. His eyes trail down the boulevard, past the Town Hall,

to a set of flower beds. Gobbledy snatches the miniature flower bed out of the village and chomps it down in
one bite.

Fi clears her throat. "I don't know if I'd leave Gobbledy up here."

I snatch him up quickly and put him back on the
sofa. "Maybe he could stay at your house."

"My sister is nosier than your dad."

"Okay, good point. Maybe you could set up some
cameras in here. I can't keep him in my room."

That gets her attention. "Hey, yeah. Let me run to
my house and see what's in the basement."

Gobbledy snuggles down into a corner of the sofa.
He looks kind of cute, actually. I grab two old blankets
from the floor. He watches me fluff them up with his
big eyes. His huge ears twitch. He stretches out, staring
at his big feet. He touches his eight toes on each foot,
one by one.

"I'm sorry I left you in the jar." I drop the blankets
into a soft pile on the sofa. "It must have been awful. I
had no idea you'd grow so much."

He rubs the corner of a blanket against his furry
cheek and chirps. After a second, he wades into the
folds of the blankets and rolls around.

"You're trouble." I point down at the village. "You
see this village?"

Gobbledy cocks his head and chirps.

"This is not food. Understand? I've got enough trouble I'm trying to get out of."

I pick up the *Encyclopedia of Animals* that Dougal dropped on the floor. I flip through page after page. Anteater. Badger. Bobcat. Horse. Indian Elephant.

Dougal runs up the stairs and drops a canvas shopping bag full of snacks on the floor. "Where'd Fi go?" "Next door, to see if she can find some equipment."

Gobbledy gets up, walks to the edge of the sofa, and smacks his lips.

I close the encyclopedia, defeated. "I can't find anything that even slightly resembles Gobbledy in this book."

Dougal rifles through the canvas bag and pulls out a loaf of bread and a jar of peanut butter. When he unscrews the lid, Gobbledy thrusts his nose in the air, taking a big, long whiff. "Dad's old laptop is in a box on the other side of the stairs."

My little brother spreads creamy peanut butter on a piece of bread with a plastic knife, adds another piece of bread to the top, and hands it to Gobbledy, who smells it, then gobbles around the edges, smacking his lips.

Smack, smack.

Sandwich gobbled in three bites.

I rifle through the canvas bag.

Three econo-packs of animal crackers.

One snack-size bag of potato chips.

A box of bran flakes.

Low-salt pretzels.

Half-eaten bag of trail mix.

Chocolate cream toaster pastry.

One glass canteen of water.

One small plastic bottle of milk.

And a bag of grapes Dad has been heckling us to eat for a week. All gobbled in record time.

Dougal makes a second peanut butter sandwich. Gobbledy claps his furry hands together, bouncing on the blanket. I open the bottle of milk and hand it over. The little thing snatches the bottle from my hand and sniffs curiously.

My eyes travel to the empty Cricket Colony jar, and I shiver.

Nine

The laptop takes forever to boot up. Gobbledy sits with his legs stretched out in front of him, scooting back and forth on the blanket. He clutches his empty milk bottle tight. Dougal reaches for it. Gobbledy squeezes, backing away.

"It's okay," Dougal reasons, "I'll put it in the recycling for you."

Slowly but deliberately, Gobbledy wraps his skinny, furry arms around the entire bottle.

"Okay," Dougal decides, "probably not a battle worth fighting."

The laptop finally beeps.

"Hopefully this thing will pull a wireless signal," Dougal says, walking over to the storage side. The attic is divided into two sections, split by the staircase: the side where Mom created a workspace, and the other side, which is for storage. A few seconds later, Dougal returns with a big smile.

He holds up an old pet carrier. "Looky what I found. Remember when we agreed to keep Fi's awful cat? We can use this for that thing you sprouted in the jar."

Gobbledy has passed out, clutching his milk bottle in one hand, his blanket in the other. When I turn my attention back to the door, the pet carrier is on the floor and Dougal is gone.

Footsteps pound up the stairs. I freeze. Gobbledy grumbles. Instinctively, I toss a blanket over him. It's only Fiona, back from her reconnaissance mission.

Fi runs to the sofa with her messenger bag. Looking at the screen of our old laptop, she raises an eyebrow, "You guys are so 1995 over here."

Dougal walks into the room holding a model volcano. "What do you know about 1995, Fi? You weren't even born."

Fi closes our laptop and sets her newer, swanky model on top. Hers fires up in seconds.

"My sister told me all about 1995. It was terrible. There was no internet."

"Dexter?" Dad calls out from the bottom of the stairs.

"Yes?" Dougal yells from the doorway.

"Anyway, umm . . . so I accidentally burned dinner while I was on another conference call with work. I'm ordering a pizza. I'll call you when it arrives."

"Order two. With double cheese," I yell.

"We're on a budget," Dad yells back.

Gobbledy's whiskers twitch while he sleeps, and I get a chance to really examine them. They're about half a foot long and stick straight out from the sides of his furry face. Fi clicks on a screen icon and pulls up a search engine. Dougal drops an armload of stuffed animals and walks over. Side by side, we all huddle around the screen.

"Do you think he's a mammal? Or she? Did you notice if it was a girl or boy?" Fi asks.

I shake my head.

"Okay. So, we have a non-gender-specific furry thing that gobbles up everything in sight, who has developed a relationship with a milk bottle," Fi says.

I nod. "That about covers it. Do you think he could be from outer space?"

Tapping the plastic laptop cover, Fi says, "Actually, he kind of looks like a stuffed animal. And. . . ."

"The rock!" I blurt out.

"And yes, he does appear to have *hatched* from a rock, if such a thing can be possible."

"Type 'golden rocks' into the search engine," I say.

Fi types and hits enter.

Dougal gives me the side eye. "Sometimes you show these flickers of brilliance that startle me."

A headline pops up:

GOLDEN ROCKS FOUND IN FOREST.

We stare in silence until Dougal taps the screen. "Click on the article."

Fi reads aloud: "Several sightings of lights falling from the sky over Pennsylvania are under investigation by a team of researchers from the Planetary Society. Residents nearby noticed the phenomenon last night and reported it to authorities. No sounds were heard, but an impact site was reported. The research team led by the Planetary Society is exploring the area for clues as to the origins of the glowing rocks, that could prove to be meteorites."

Fi copies and pastes the name and does a search for the society.

A second later, results pop up on the screen.

"The Planetary Society is just a few hours away. Do you think we should call them?" I ask.

Dougal actually turns all the way around to look at me. Not a good sign.

"We could sneak into Dad's office and use the video cam like we do when we talk to G-daddy and G-mama."

Dougal shakes his head. "The rule is no calling strangers without permission, and no going into Dad's study. Ever."

Gobbledy squeezes his milk bottle, rolls over, and starts snoring.

Dougal points at the storage area and whispers, "Go see if you can find something to keep him entertained when he wakes up."

I nod and walk over to the storage side. I spot my old plastic toy shopping cart. I smile. When Fi and I were little, we put her cat, Sir Shreds-A-Lot, in the shopping basket and took him for rides. I push the handle, watching it roll. It might be a nice place for an alien life form to play. Next, I come across a box marked with the label, "Building Blocks and Legos." Mom was an organizational freak. Her words, not mine. I fill the shopping cart with building blocks and Legos and roll it over to the other side.

Fi is hunched over the laptop, scrolling through photos of small, furry creatures. I hold up a toy and squeak it. Gobbledy awakens and lifts his head.

I smile. "He likes it."

I set the toy on the blanket. Gobbledy sniffs, then jumps up and down on it.

Squeak squeak squeak.

Dougal eyes the little beast.

"What is that noise," Dad yells up from the bottom of the stairs.

Dougal snatches Gobbledy up with both hands. The room goes silent.

Clearing his throat, Dougal yells down, "Dexter is playing with an old toy."

"Oh. Well, tell him to stop being so OCD about it."

Obsessive-Compulsive Disorder. Our dad, the psychologist.

I pull my lips into a tight frown. "Why do you *always* blame everything on me?"

"Who got us into this mess?" Dougal asks, setting Gobbledy down carefully with one hand and snatching the toy away with the other. A deep, horrific yowl erupts from Gobbledy. Dougal quickly hands the toy back. *Squeak squeak squeak* goes the toy, as Gobbledy cuts his eyes at Dougal.

Fi unzips a duffel bag and pulls out gadgets, laying

each one on the sofa. "I'll set up some surveillance in here. I have four cameras left. I'll put one in each corner." Pinching her brow, she looks around the attic. "I might be able to pull some audio, too."

Dougal stares at her. "You might be able to get into college now if you ask."

Fi laughs. "I excel at spying, but not so much at World and Its People."

Gobbledy sits on the sofa, his skinny legs stretched out in front of him, watching Fi. He's awfully cute looking with his skinny legs and long whiskers. I am really starting to wonder where he came from. "What if he did come from outer space?"

Fi plugs a power cord into the wall. "That's what I think." She points a playful finger at Gobbledy and clicks her tongue twice.

Gobbledy does the same thing.

Fi claps her hands. "Listen here, Galactic Gobbledy, I need you to figure out a way to tell us where you're from."

Ten

Dougal seizes the opportunity to turn the laptop around. "Okay," he says, "we're going to send an email to the Planetary Society. What do you think it should say?"

Gobbledy turns his back to us, hunches over, grunts like he's going to the bathroom, and drops a grape on the sofa. *Thump.*

Dougal looks at me. "Did you teach him that?"

I shake my head.

Gobbledy squeals with delight, grunts, hunches over, and drops another grape on the sofa like he's pooping fruit.

Dougal clicks on the contact form for the Planetary Society. "Small alien thing, good sense of humor, knows how to poop grapes, non-gender-specific, possibly mammalian, has developed healthy relationship with milk bottle and my brother. Found in the forest near our house. May be a rock. Send help now."

Fi nods, "That about covers it."

Dougal hits send. "So, what about that plan?"

Dad yells from the downstairs hall, "Pizza's here."

Ready to sink my teeth into double cheese, I launch myself forward. "I'll go."

Dougal slaps his hand on my chest. "I will go. You will tend to the little beast."

Fi walks to her open laptop. "Three pieces for me, please."

"Dream on," Dougal snorts. "Have you met our dad?"

"I have, and while he is very uptight and sometimes falling apart, I have nothing but love for Mr. D.," she says, simultaneously typing on her keyboard.

Dougal raises his eyebrows. "I'll see if your appreciation can score you a slice."

The sound of Dougal clomping down the stairs is highlighted by images popping onto Fi's screen.

It takes me a second, but then suddenly I know what I am looking at. "That's our attic."

Fi smiles and points to one quad on the screen. "And that is our small friend there."

On screen, Gobbledy looks up. He cocks his head and chirps.

"Come over here," Fi says.

It takes him a second but finally Gobbledy stands and walks over to Fi's end of the sofa.

"We can see you onscreen," she says. "It will help us protect you."

Gobbledy leans closer and closer, until he wobbles on the edge. Then he touches the screen. He stares at the screen, blinking. He taps the screen, then touches his furry chest.

"Do you know what those rocks are?" I ask him.

He points to himself.

Fi's jaw drops open. "He understands you!"

If that's true, Gobbledy is the first thing on the planet to understand me.

"Ask him again," she urges.

Gobbledy presses a key on Fi's laptop and stares at the screen. I stop to watch. There is something so different about the way his bright, moss-green eyes watch Fi.

Gobbledy points at the screen.

Fi looks over. "What is it?"

Gobbledy taps the screen with his furry finger. Fi and I lean forward, squinting. "What is it?"

I can't tell what he's pointing at, but suddenly Fi whispers, "*The rocks.*"

Turning to face her, his head bobs up and down.

She inches forward on the sofa. He points to the screen again.

"Gobbledy," I say, "do you know what those things are?"

He nods and points to himself again.

In a low, thoughtful whisper, Fi asks, "What if they're not rocks? What if they're *eggs*?"

"But they would have all hatched."

"Not necessarily. Even eggs need certain temperatures, elements, and fertilization to hatch. Maybe it was those electric mushrooms."

Gobbledy leans in close, touching the screen with his little furry hand. His fingers trace the rocks. He looks back at us, then at the screen again.

Footsteps pound up the stairs, and I am ready to hide Gobbledy when Dougal rounds the corner balancing a stack of three paper plates with two slices of pizza each.

"You have to see this," Fi says, rushing him over.

I reach for a plate of steaming hot, yummy good pizza, as Dougal walks to the other side of Fi and crouches down to look at the screen. Gobbledy tosses his head back and takes a long whiff. I set my plate in my lap. Gobbledy grabs my plate and eats the entire thing. Pizza *and* paper plate.

"What have you done?" I yell.

"Stop fighting!" Dad yells from the upstairs hall.

"I—I . . . umm. Okay!" I yell back.

All eyes in the room turn to Gobbledy. He smacks his lips.

Dougal shrugs. "He's smart."

"What?"

"All smart people love pizza," he says, sinking his teeth into one of the two slices on this plate. Gobbledy runs down the table and reaches for the second slice on his plate. Dougal slaps his hand. Gobbledy growls. Dougal leans forward, face to furry face, and growls back.

Fi snaps her fingers. "Dougal, you need to see this. Gobbledy," she says, "what are these rocks?"

Gobbledy eyes Dougal, but points to himself.

"Whoa. What?" Dougal's jaw drops open. "He understands you?"

Fi goes on, "Okay, say they are eggs. They would have a life expectancy just like anything else. So what do you think that missing link is?"

I consider my lab under the stairs. "Well, there's no natural light, just drops of water to keep the jars humid. Warm, kinda nice, if I do say so myself."

"Listen, Gobbledy may be proof that life exists on other planets."

My little brother shakes his head. "How do we know he isn't some undiscovered species on this planet?"

Fi inhales deep. "Okay. Good point. We'll do some research."

My stomach growls. Like the living picture of cool she is, Fi hands me a piece of her pizza. I snarf it down.

Fi chews, looking around the room. Gobbledy jumps into her lap, reaching for her slice of pizza. Fi holds it higher, out of his reach. He grabs his milk bottle and thumps his foot.

"What do you think he's saying?" I ask.

Dougal glances at me out of the corner of his eye. "He's saying he is a tragically cute alien life form who is going to get you grounded for the rest of your life."

Gobbledy wakes Fi's laptop up and presses the keys. The video starts playing.

"You want to go get the rocks, don't you?" Fi asks.

Now we have Dougal's full attention. "We are not filling up the attic with little gobbledy things."

"Maybe he has a family somewhere," Fi offers. "Maybe he was a teeny egg Dexter scooped up and hatched in that jar. Maybe he has a family in the forest worried about him. We should at least check."

Gobbledy bounces nervously, pointing at the screen.

"Maybe we should take him now," I suggest.

Dougal's mouth actually falls open. "Are you totally nuts? It's dark outside. You've already gotten in trouble once today. What is it about rules that you don't understand?"

Gobbledy tosses his head back and lets out a low wail. Fi touches him on his furry shoulder, and when he looks at her, he falls silent, whiskers twitching.

Covering his face with his hands, Dougal mumbles, "Does it have to be now?"

Eleven

Fifteen minutes later, Fi says with authority, "Flashlight?"

I am in charge of verifying supplies. "Check."

"Compass?"

Gobbledy grabs the compass from the table, turning around in a circle, watching the dial.

My annoying little brother clears his throat. "We don't have all night. Water canteen?"

"Technically, we do," Fi says. "Tomorrow is Saturday."

"I like my sleep, Fiona," Dougal growls.

Trying to get the research party back on track, I say cheerfully, "Check."

Dougal stuffs my night-vision goggles into the backpack and gives me the stink eye. "I can't believe I let you two talk me into this."

Fi comes to my rescue. "You can stay here."

I pull my ninja Halloween costume on from last year. It was in a box on the other side of the attic. If we're going to sneak out, I'm going to do it right. Dexter Ninja.

Tired of waiting, Gobbledy plops down on the sofa and unwraps a peanut butter and jelly sandwich. He chews the crust thoughtfully, then gobbles his way to the center. Strawberry jam clings to his long whiskers.

"Why do you guys have twelve new jars of peanut butter downstairs?" Fi asks.

"Mom used to do all the shopping. Dad doesn't know how to shop. He buys a case of everything."

Fi raises an eyebrow. "That explains the twenty-four light bulbs next to the three cases of cheese crackers in the pantry."

Gobbledy rips open a bag of cheese crackers with his teeth.

"He's very resourceful," Dougal observes. "Maybe he'll stay in the forest and live in the trees."

Fi rolls her eyes. "That's mean."

"Then maybe he should live at your house, because at our house we have rules."

Fi shrugs, "I would, but Dexter found him, and Sir Shreds would eat him."

While they argue, I stare at Gobbledy's long, skinny legs and huge feet. I love his big, moss-colored eyes and his long whiskers and eyebrows. I love his skinny, hairy fingers, and big ears with huge tufts of fur on the tips. Soft and funny, he is way cuter than any animal I've ever seen. And I have seen a lot of them.

Touching his hairy toes, Fi says, "I wish I could scan you."

Gobbledy chatters loudly.

"Shh." Dougal says.

Standing up on his skinny, wobbly legs, Gobbledy

points at the grainy, green night-vision on Fi's screen. He grabs another sandwich, and when Dougal tries to take it away Gobbledy eats the whole thing, plastic bag and all.

"At the rate he's eating, he'll be the size of a Saint Bernard in a few weeks," Fi observes.

"Or less." I shrug, unwilling to consider how I could ever hide anything that big.

Dougal grabs collection cups from his science kit, tongs, bug catcher, sifting basket, and a pair of rubber gloves. He inventories each piece before stuffing it in his backpack. He stares at Gobbledy. "Try not to contaminate the samples."

Gobbledy sits down on the edge of the table with a bag of granola.

Crunch. Crunch. Crunch.

Dougal lifts his eyes from his list. "Emergency glow light?"

I shove the glow light in the backpack, and hold it open for Gobbledy to climb inside. He clutches his empty milk bottle and steps in. I leave the top unzipped, so he has room to breathe.

I hoist the pack onto my back and walk down the dark staircase, listening to his soft chirps and squeaks. The night light glows in the hall. We quietly pass Dad's room, stopping briefly to listen. Satisfied with silence, we walk to the first floor and out the kitchen door. Sir Shreds-A-Lot is on the back porch, flicking his tail. He growls and hisses in the moonlight.

Fi shoos the cat away. "Be quiet. You'll wake everyone up."

We avoid the second and fifth steps, because they squeak. The moon is brilliant and full, a perfect white light washing the world in a silver glow. The cold air brushes away my yawn. Shadows slant across the driveway, down to the curb where the last few fallen leaves skitter in the breeze. Gobbledy raises up behind me, chirping and squeaking. His furry little hands squeeze my neck tight. We set off on foot, sticking to the shadows.

Twelve

The entrance to the forest is dark. The only time I've been in the forest at night was when Fi and I went looking for Sir Shreds-A-Lot, who ended up being locked in their garage. Not only is it pitch black, it's super quiet. My stomach twists and turns in knots. Fi, Dougal, Gobbledy, and I stand at the edge of the playground, staring into the dark rows of trees.

Dougal pulls out his flashlight. "Okay, let's get this over with."

Gobbledy clucks loud and fast, like a car engine revving up.

Dougal glances back over his shoulder. "See, he likes it here. We could visit if he decides to stay."

Fi crinkles up her nose, and frowns. "What is with him?" She reaches behind me, and even though I can't see, I know she's scratching Gobbledy's head. "This could be the most important discovery of our life, and all he does is act like a grouch."

I straighten my ninja outfit and sigh. "He's always been weird, but since Mom died, he acts like he has to follow every single rule, or Dad will freak out."

It's Fi's turn to sigh. "He thinks that by doing certain things or acting a certain way, he can bring her back. I did that. I thought if I laid my clothes out every single night like my mom did, then someone would feel bad and give her back to me."

Dougal disappears into the dark tree line. "Let's get this mission underway," he yells.

Gobbledy chatters.

"Dark forest at night really isn't my thing," I admit.

Fi shrugs. "It's not mine, either, but it doesn't matter," she says, pointing at Gobbledy. "This is for him."

I click on my flashlight.

Gobbledy chatters constantly as we hike back to where Fi set up her cameras. I set my backpack carefully on the ground. Gobbledy jumps out, landing with an impressive *thud*. Standing in a stream of moonlight, he squishes dirt in between his many toes. The silver glow illuminates his furry body as he holds his arms out to the side, inhales, and squishes.

I kneel down and touch the soft, sandy earth that winds down to the river.

"Umm, Dexter, was this here before?"

Dougal points his flashlight at a charred strip of earth. Fi hunkers down snapping photos with her flash, blinding me.

I shrug. "I don't know. Maybe. We were kind of in a hurry." Turning in a circle, I realize, "We didn't go this far."

Dougal touches the burnt end of a log. Fi falls back

on her heels, tilting her flashlight up into the treetops.

Pointing a stream of light at singed branches, she says, "I think Gobbledy came from out there."

"From the sky?"

Fi tilts her head way back. "Or farther."

Seconds tick by as I consider this information. "Do you mean outer space?"

"Yes, though I prefer the term 'galactic.'"

I look up through the treetops to the sky, to the great beyond. If Fiona is right, and she is usually always right, then this is the discovery of a lifetime.

"Dexter?"

I lower my eyes, looking straight at Dougal.

He points behind me. When I turn, I see Gobbledy on his knees, searching under piles of leaves. Fi walks over, giving him light.

After a second, she says, "The mushrooms are gone."

Gobbledy pushes leaves away with his skinny fingers. No glowing rocks. No mushrooms, either. Fi kneels down, helping him clear away the leaves.

"What mushrooms?" Dougal asks.

"There were these weird mushroom tree-like things, but they're not here anymore."

Suddenly, Gobbledy finds a rock, snatching it up quick.

"Do you want me to put this in my pack?" I ask.

Gobbledy shakes his head. A second later, he releases his grip. The rock lands on the ground with a thump. He walks past the charred log, frantically moving from rock to rock, touching each one. His skinny legs wobble in the cold.

Dougal pulls his collection cups out. "What's going on, guys?"

"There's something wrong with the other rocks. They're different than the ones Fi and I saw."

Dark tree branches are etched across the night sky by the light of the moon. The smell of dirt and old leaves is strong. Silver light pours through the leafless branches. Fi holds her hands out, palms up. Three rocks sit on each palm, along with a shriveled-up mushroom. Glancing at Gobbledy, her mouth pinches tight, and I hear the quiver in her voice. "I don't think these are alive anymore."

Gobbledy's furry chin falls to his chest.

"Okay, wait," Fi says frantically. "There were many rocks."

Pushing leaves away with his big, skinny feet, Gobbledy keeps looking, but the way his shoulders hunch forward suggests he doesn't expect to find anything. I look over at Dougal, who hasn't said anything.

Fi's eyes shimmer in the light. "Let's each start looking for rocks. Right now. We can gather samples later." Sweeping Gobbledy up and setting him on her shoulder, she searches the ground.

For a split second, Gobbledy stops sulking, and Fi stops moving leaves. In that precious silence, we can all hear something walking toward us on the path. The soft *whomp* of footsteps and the crackle of dried leaves.

"Shh . . ." Dougal says. "Someone is coming."

Gobbledy climbs down Fi's arm and runs deep into the grove of trees. I can't see him anymore.

In the dark, Gobbledy wails long and loud.

My little brother yells, "Make him stop!"

In one direction, I hear something walking down the path toward us. In the opposite direction, I hear Gobbledy sobbing and pushing leaves away.

"Turn your flashlights off," Fi whispers loudly.

I click mine off and listen. "Maybe it's a jogger," I whisper back.

Gobbledy ignores us, digging.

Dougal whispers, barely loud enough to hear. "I hope Dad didn't follow us. This will be Code Red for sure."

Dougal moves closer to me. Even in the dark, I can hear the creak of his backpack strap. The footsteps stop. No one moves. Finally, Fi clicks her flashlight on and points it in the direction of the path. A tail flicks in the light. Sir Shreds-A-Lot stands on the dirt path, staring in the direction of Gobbledy.

Fi groans. "What are you doing out here? I put you in the basement."

Sir Shreds twitches his tail and crouches down, like a ferocious lion on TV.

Sensing danger, Gobbledy stops digging. I run over to him, and he grabs the flashlight out of my hand.

"I can't believe this cat," Fi huffs.

"He must have followed us from the back porch," Dougal says.

Gobbledy searches the ground frantically.

Keeping one eye on the cat, I help. None of the rocks look anything like they did earlier. The rock I put in my Cricket Colony glowed golden. With tears in his eyes and big sniffles, Gobbledy searches.

"Where are you going?" Fi yells.

"I'm following Gobbledy," I yell back, watching his skinny legs wobble as he runs for the river.

The water is black, even under the moonlight. I stop at a row of pine trees. Gobbledy stumbles down the muddy bank.

"Hey, I need a flashlight!"

The thud of shoes hitting the ground is the only thing I hear until Dougal and Fi's flashlights cut a path. Dougal sweeps his light across the river, while Fi holds hers in place with one hand, and clutches Sir Shreds in the other.

It takes me a minute, but my eyes finally adjust to the bright burst of light in the dark. Down at the edge of the water, Gobbledy stands, pointing to a piece of metal jutting up from the mud.

"*Oh, my god*," Fi whispers. "Is that what I think it is?" Shreds hisses loudly and wiggles in her arms. "Listen, someone pick up Gobbledy so I can let go of this deranged cat."

"I will." I walk down to the water's edge. My feet sink in the mud. My tennis shoes make a loud sucking noise as I take each step. Once I'm close enough, I lift Gobbledy in the air. He points down at the piece of metal, glinting in the flashlight. Cold mud seeps up to my ankles.

Dougal stands at the top of the embankment. "We need to get back."

Gobbledy tries to wiggle free.

"Hey," I say, squeezing tight. "You can't stay out here alone."

Tossing his head back, he lets out the saddest wail I've ever heard.

"Listen," I say firmly. "You're going home with us. We will work this out."

Using his back legs, Gobbledy pushes off my chest and makes a run for the place where we found the rocks.

Sir Shreds runs after him.

Dougal groans loudly and runs after both.

I stand ankle deep in mud. "Fi, I need some help."

By the time I crest the embankment, Dougal has Gobbledy in his arms, with Shreds weaving in and out of his legs, circling like a shark. My feet slip around inside my tennis shoes, making it hard to run. My teeth are chattering.

"Look, we can't stay out here much longer. My nosy sister gets up early on Saturday for yoga," Fi says.

I am so cold my whole body starts to shake.

"We've obviously found a piece of his craft," Dougal says, pointing down to the river.

Clouds pass in front of the moon. The sudden dark is black and cold. I clench my jaw, so I don't look like a baby standing in the forest at night, trying to uncover the mystery of a lifetime with my teeth chattering.

Gobbledy uses my flashlight to look over Dougal's shoulder. Light sweeps across patches of dry dirt and leaves. None of the rocks glow. Gobbledy wails, his head falling on Dougal's shoulder.

"We can fix this," I blurt out.

Even in the dark I can see Dougal shaking his head.

"Dexter's right," Fi jumps in. "We can. We just need to know more about what we're dealing with. Look, we've got the cameras set up. Let's get back, and I'll look for more clues."

Gobbledy reaches for me, his soft fur brushing against my arm.

"We can help you," I whisper. He clamors over to me, and I hold him tight and walk back to my pack.

Dougal huffs in the most exasperated way. "You don't know that! We don't know anything about these rocks. We don't know what they are, or where they're from."

Fi tosses her backpack over her shoulder. "We'll meet back up in the morning and figure this out."

Thirteen

Bare branches scrape against the bedroom window, dragging me from sleep. I open my eyes. A thick, gray sky foretells of winter. Across the room, Dougal is bunched up in his rocket ship sleeping bag, snoring. Since the whole thing with Mom happened, he's been sleeping in my room.

"Psst!"

More snoring. For someone so small, he sure can make a lot of noise. His nostrils flare, and his bottom lip trembles. I climb out of bed. My mud-covered tennis shoes are on the floor, still wet.

"Psst!" I whisper again, louder.

Snoring.

I roll my eyes and throw my pillow at his head.

He lurches forward. "Wha?"

"Hurry up. We've got to meet up with Fi."

Dougal's eyes drift to the window, then the digital clock: 7:17. His head flops back onto my pillow, and he gives me the stink eye. "It's Saturday, you freak. We have all day."

I pull on my fleece pants and dig around in the closet

for a pair of shoes that fit and aren't covered in mud. "I'm going to check on Gobbledy. I'll meet you downstairs. We've got to get over to Fi's."

When I crest the top of the stairs and walk through the door to the attic, I find Gobbledy sitting on the sofa, staring down at his hairy knees.

Exactly the way I left him.

Shoulders hunched forward, he lifts his head to look at me.

I sit next to him on the sofa. "Look, I'm gonna help you with this. Dad has to work today. We'll have the house to ourselves."

Gobbledy sighs, long and deep.

I pull the canvas bag of food closer. Thrusting my hand inside, I pull out a bagel.

Gobbledy shakes his head.

"Toaster tart?" I ask. "Banana?"

I can't stand to see him so sad. He might have come a very long way. To think all that time ended in sadness is depressing. I unscrew a jar of peanut butter. His ears perk up, but only slightly.

"Dexter?" Dad yells up the stairs.

I freeze in place. Dad is supposed to be at work. "Listen, I gotta go downstairs but I'll be back soon."

"Dexter?" Dad yells again.

"Coming," I yell back.

I grab a box of stuffed animals and a sleeping bag. Bunching them all together, I make a comfy nest on the sofa. He lets me lift him up and place him in the middle. I hand him his milk bottle. "Wait right here for me."

Gobbledy wraps his arms around the milk bottle and closes his eyes.

"Dexter?" Dad yells, sounding so totally annoyed that I run for the stairs.

"I've gotta go," I whisper. "Stay up here."

I run down the attic steps two at a time. At the bottom, I try to get the door to latch, but it's broken. Everything is falling apart with Mom gone and Dad working all the time.

Dad is pouring coffee when I breeze into the kitchen, trying to look like I'm not hiding something in the attic.

He slams his cup on the counter. "Son, what in the world is wrong with you? I've been calling you for ten minutes."

Surprise number one, he's supposed to be at work. Instead, he's hanging around the kitchen severely annoyed. He can do that at work. Dougal raises his eyebrow and walks into the pantry to avoid eye contact.

Dad's body slumps into a relaxation breath. Exhale to a count of ten, nine, eight . . . I can hear the guided meditation playing down the hall when he's had a bad day. At zero, he inhales and says, "After I went to bed last night, I realized we'd forgotten something huge."

Sir Shreds scratches at the back door, letting out a long, solemn meow.

I look from the back door to Dad, and ask, "What did we forget?"

Dad exhales. "We forgot a tree."

"We've got one out back," I say, reaching for a bag of pretzels on the counter to feed my growling stomach.

"A Kissmas tree," Dad says.

Reality washes over me. We've done nothing for Kissmas. Mom was the leader of the Kiss. Without her leading the charge, we are almost to winter break with no sign of Kissmas in our house.

"I've been so busy with work," Dad says.

I nod. "It's okay."

"So I was thinking—" Dad says.

Before he can finish, I blurt out, "I've got to go next door and help Fi with a project."

"Can't it wait?" Dad asks.

The cat meows outside the door, tearing the wood with his claws. *Yeoooooow.*

Dad frowns, glancing at the door, then back to me. "So I thought we could all go pick one out together."

I fidget with a loose string on my fleece pants, trying to think of any way to get out of leaving Gobbledy alone.

"Oh, come on," Dad says. "It'll be fun."

Meow!

Dad walks over to the back door and looks down. "What's gotten into this cat?"

I can tell the relaxation breath is wearing off.

"Listen," I say. "I'll take the cat next door and tell Fi I'll be over later."

Tension melts from Dad's body. He rolls back on his heels. "Sounds like a plan."

Dougal frowns.

Before anyone has a chance to object, I open the door and grab the angry cat.

Sir Shreds is the most obnoxious, squirmy cat I've ever met. Fi opens the door in her pajamas. Her minty breath lingers in the cold morning air. "Hey, I've been watching my live feeds looking for clues."

I hand over the cat.

"How does he keep getting out?" she asks, crinkling up her nose.

"Listen," I say, quickly. "We've got to go pick out a Christmas tree."

"Now?"

I nod. "Mom used to get everyone excited about this stuff."

Fi sighs. "We need to inspect that piece of craft."

"I'll be back as soon as possible. Listen, see if you can contact the Planetary Society. We might need help."

The kitchen is warm and smells like cinnamon buns. My stomach growls.

"What do you want me to say?"

"Just see if you can get someone on the phone."

Fi grabs a weird phone off the counter.

"What is that?"

"It's a satellite phone. Daddy bought it for when he's traveling, but now it just lies around the house."

"Why are you so cool that you have a satellite phone?"

She shrugs. "Just lucky, I guess."

She spins a laptop around on the counter, and a grainy video of our attic fills the screen. At first, I don't know what I am looking at. Then, I realize Gobbledy is sitting on the sofa holding the Pet Rock Dad got me. Gobbledy holds up the small cardboard carrier with the holes in the top. Staring down into the box, he pokes the Pet Rock with a finger.

"How long has he been staring at my Pet Rock?"

"Since you left the attic."

"We have to figure out a way to help him."

I lean forward, squinting at the computer screen. "He's so funny-looking."

Fi crinkles her nose and laughs. "I know. He's very cute. I checked on him a few times during the night."

"What was he doing?"

"Looking at your mom's village on the table, sitting alone on the sofa, looking out the broken window." Lowering her voice, she leans in close. "I think he's a lot smarter than we're giving him credit for."

"Why?"

"Just a hunch."

A horn honks in our driveway. "Listen, I gotta go."

"I can't believe you're ditching me."

"Postponing." I jerk my thumb towards our attic. "Keep an eye on him."

The horn honks again.

"Got it." Fi says, handing me a cinnamon bun.

"Life saver," I whisper, saluting her with my free hand.

"I know," she says.

Fourteen

Dad parks in the lot next to the playground. Dougal and I exchange a look.

Grabbing an axe from the passenger seat, Dad steps out of the station wagon. The air is sharp and chilly, the sky a translucent gray. Crows caw from the treetops, swooping down to brown patches of grass.

Dad tosses the axe over one shoulder, walking towards the row of trees. "Let's go," he calls back to us.

Dougal and I get out of the car. "Umm . . . Dad . . . what exactly are we doing?"

Without stopping, he yells back, "There's a grove of pine trees along the river. It was your mom's favorite place to walk with me." A second later, he disappears into the forest.

"Oh, my god," Dougal says. "He's headed straight for that piece of craft stuck in the mud."

"Why is our father suddenly cutting down trees?" I wail.

Dougal huffs, loud and annoyed. "Because he misses Mom." Pushing me forward, he breaks into a run. "We have to stop him before he gets to the clearing."

I wipe my sticky cinnamon fingers on my pants and launch into a sprint. There's no way I'm letting Dad stumble onto our discovery. He'll call the news and tell everyone. Then, a bunch of adults will show up and take credit. I run at a frantic pace. By the time I catch up to Dad, he is standing on the path, staring at Dougal like he's crazy.

Turning his attention to me, he asks, "What's going on with you two?"

"What if we don't want a tree?" I blurt out.

Dad looks at *me* like I'm crazy.

Dougal dives in for the save. "I mean, what if someone lives in the tree we cut down?"

Judging by the look on Dad's face, this has never occurred to him. He clears his throat nervously, arms falling to his sides. The heavy axe tip hits the ground.

Dougal points out, "I mean, what if animals live in the tree, but are out gathering food? When they return, their house will be gone!"

Puffs of air flare from Dad's nostrils. "Are you serious?"

We nod vigorously, quite possibly the first time we've been in total agreement.

"What if we can find an unoccupied tree?" Dad offers.

Dad loves logic. I am certain logic will keep him out of the forest, so I ask, "How can we be sure?"

He inhales. "Well, let's think about it. How can we be sure it's vacant?"

Dougal shrugs. "We can't. Besides, what are we going to do with the tree?"

"We decorate it," Dad says, matter of fact. "You know that."

"Then what?" Dougal presses.

"After Christmas we drag it out to the curb and the city picks it up and puts it in the woodchipper."

A cold breeze blows through the forest. Leaves tremble.

"The woodchipper?" Dougal raises an eyebrow.

Squirrels run across branches overhead. An acorn drops to the ground with an impressive thump. I look down. Half-concealed under leaves, a small, golden rock glows inches from my feet, inside a ring of electric mushrooms.

"But we came all the way out here to get a tree. If you had moral objections, they should have been voiced when we were in the kitchen," Dad squeezes the axe handle, irked.

"I won't do it," Dougal says, firmly. "I won't send a tree to the woodchipper. We must leave the forest right now."

As my dad and brother argue about a tree, my eyes search the ground. One glowing rock definitely shimmers beneath the fallen leaves. I just have to get it in my pocket without anyone noticing.

Dad spins around and points his axe at a small spruce. "Okay, maybe not a pine. How about this one?"

Dougal follows the axe with his eyes, turning his back on me. "Absolutely not," he says.

"That one?"

I swoop down fast and grab the rock. It shocks the crap out of me, but I get it in my hand. It's warm as I shove it in my pocket. Quickly, I dust my hands off, and try to avoid looking guilty by making a helpful suggestion. "Can't we just buy a fake tree?"

Dad sighs. "We are on a budget."

"I'll put my allowance toward a fake tree," I blurt out.

"So will I," Dougal says.

I need my allowance more than ever, but I'll do anything to get Dad away from glowing rocks and scorched earth and surveillance cameras that lead back to a life form living in our attic, which leads straight to Code Red.

Lotta Dollar is a madhouse. After circling the lot like a shark, we finally find a parking space. Dad groans and shoves open the car door. It is not the sound of triumph. Holiday shoppers parade up and down the sidewalks, lugging bags.

Dougal walks straight into the center of chaos like a boss. "Let's go."

Mismatched stockings and broken candy canes dangle from strings. It's pretty obvious that the best of Christmas has been strip-mined from this store.

We pass towers of mops, sponges, coat hangers, tape, and bathroom cleaner to stop in front of a small display of tree skirts and ornaments in dented boxes.

Not a tree in sight.

We look left, then right.

Dougal turns in a complete circle. "Does anyone see a fake tree?"

I shake my head. The rock is warm in my pocket. I want to tell him, but he still seems pretty bothered by the first rock. It's hard to gauge his moods these days.

While I am contemplating whether to let my little brother in on the new development, Dad flags down a passing saleswoman. "Excuse me, do you have any more Christmas trees?"

She purses her lips together in a way that does not instill hope. "Let's see. If we've got any, they'll be over here with the dust mops. You're cutting it a little close aren't you, mister?"

Dad nods sheepishly, afraid of being reprimanded by a saleswoman with a name tag that reads "Gertie."

"Hmm . . ." She bends over, pushing boxes out of the way. Grunting under her breath, she finally rises up with a triumphant, "Got one!"

Crammed in between a display of dust mops and Green Clean is the most dented box I've ever seen. Gertie drags the box into the middle of the aisle and rips the tape off the cardboard flap with her teeth. "Hey, it looks like you're in for a deal." Spinning the box around, she points to the "fifty percent off" sticker.

Judging by the looks of the box, it should have a "free" sticker.

She lowers her voice. "Oh, goodness."

Dougal crinkles his noise in disbelief. "What is it?"

Gertie sighs. "It looks like this is one of our designer models."

Dad raises an eyebrow. "That's a good thing, right?"

Gertie thrusts her hand into the box and pulls out a gnarled, faux tree branch.

Dad shivers. "It's pink."

"Yep." She jams the pink branch back into the box. "This year they came in ice blue, purple, and pink. This is the last one. Lucky you." With a hearty nudge to the ribs, Gertie laughs. "Want me to have it gift-wrapped for you?"

Reaching for the box, Dad pulls a tight frown across his face. "We'll take it as-is."

Fifteen

The station wagon croaks. Christmas carols crackle from the plastic speakers. I'm inhaling a box of grape Nerds when Dougal smacks me hard in the chest, and I spew candy all over the back of the seat.

"What?" I growl under my breath.

Fi runs across her front yard, frantically waving her arms. When I finally make eye contact, she jerks her thumb up to our house.

I lean over, craning my neck to look out the window. She makes all these weird hand gestures and pinches her forehead tight, like she does when she's worried.

A Nerd goes down the wrong way, and I choke.

Dad looks at me in the rearview mirror. "Dexter, what now?"

I swallow and manage to croak, "Red-breasted robin in the birch tree."

"Oh," Dad says. "Kinda late in the season for robins."

As soon as he lowers his eyes from the mirror, I mouth the words, *This can't be good* to Dougal.

Dad turns into the driveway, and I press the button to release my seat belt.

As soon as the station wagon comes to a complete stop, Fi jerks my door open, yells, "Afternoon, Mr. D.," and pulls me out of the car. I abandon my bag of candy and run, ignoring Dad's calls to come help him with the pink tree monstrosity.

"What is going on?"

Fi grabs my hand and we run over to her front yard and stand behind the mulberry bush. "Somehow Gobbledy got out on the roof," Fi says, breathlessly.

My eyes shoot to the roof, but I don't see anything, "Okay. So, we'll lure him back in." Before she says another word, I know what happened. The broken latch on the attic window made it flap in the breeze, and he crawled out.

Dougal joins us behind the bushes, turning in all directions. "What is that noise?"

I stop talking and listen. "Traffic?"

"Yeah. So, what's with all of the tires squealing and honking?"

I love a good disaster as much as anyone. But the truth is I have my own disaster. Gobbledy on the roof means no sunny shores. No pirate's gold. The future is one long dirty look from my dad and Code Red forever.

Honk. Honk. Honk. Honk.

"I think Gobbledy went back to the forest," Fi says.

"*What?* I thought you said he was on the roof?"

"That's how he got out. I saw him on the cameras, but he's not up there anymore. I checked."

Deep inside his brain, Dougal zeroes in on certain

situations, particularly when it involves trouble. That look creeps into his eyes. "I am going to check this out." He runs toward the main intersection. The one we are forbidden to cross.

Dad yells, "Where is everyone going?"

"Be right back," I yell, breaking into a run.

Dougal runs towards the honking. Fi and I finally catch up. The side streets are quiet. Occasionally, we pass a car pulling into a driveway, or a person sitting on a front porch. It's pretty normal and relaxed, except for all the noise. Then we round the corner of the big intersection at Main and Third, and I almost have a heart attack.

It takes Dougal a second. Then he gasps, and slaps his hand over his mouth, mumbling, "Oh, my god. . . ." in a way that gives me chills.

"Dexter," he yells. "*Do something!*"

I appreciate the vote of confidence, but the idea that I can actually do something is highly unrealistic.

Dougal furrows his brow so tight his eyes cross. "Do something," he repeats, slapping my arm. "I thought you said he'd stay in the attic if we built him a habitat."

I look out into the intersection where Gobbledy stands, small and helpless, cars whizzing past, as he clutches an armload of rocks from the forest.

"What is he doing?" Dougal wails.

"He obviously went back to the forest to get the rocks."

"He can't do that," Dougal yells. "Why is this happening?" He swings around and jams his bony finger into my chest. "You did this."

"Stop blaming me," I yell back.

"Stop fighting," Fi yells at both of us.

Gobbledy howls. Car tires swoosh dangerously close to his fur.

Dougal opens his mouth to yell at me, then clamps it shut, growling, "He needs a cage."

Cars screech. Horns blare. I jerk my eyes back to the crisis at hand.

Dougal grabs his head, pulls his hair and wails again. "How are we supposed to get him when we can't go into the street?"

Desperate measures call for desperate acts. *Think. Think,* I urge my brain.

Dougal looks around frantically. "Dad cannot see this."

Gobbledy swings around and sees us. His eyes go wild and he yowls. The traffic light turns red. Seconds tick. The cars file forward, picking up speed. Gobbledy closes his eyes tight and squeezes his rocks.

Fi squeezes her hands together. "I can run home and call my sister."

"We don't have time. He'll have to come to us," I blurt out.

"Right." Dougal spins around immediately. He cups his hands around his mouth and yells, "Get out of the street."

Gobbledy hugs his rocks and screams.

Dougal spins around to face me. "What's Plan B?"

Food. Gobbledy loves food. I reach for Dougal's bag of candy in his hand. That's when I remember what I hid in my pocket.

Slowly, I pull the rock out.

"No," he bounces up and down, seeing the rock in my hand. "Where did you get that?" My little brother's eyes are as wide as his glasses. "Do not show him that rock. We need a Plan C. Proceed directly to Plan C."

"There is no Plan C," I yell back. "This is it."

He lunges for the rock, but I am fast, and raise it high in the air. "Gobbledy," I yell.

An SUV drives right over him as he ducks, clutching his rocks.

I hold the glowing rock higher. Gobbledy focuses, and then his eyes go wild. His big feet start running.

"Wait," Fi yells, thrusting her hand out.

We all keep one eye on Gobbledy, the other on the stoplight. Oncoming traffic turns yellow, then red.

"Run," we yell at the same time.

There is a three second delay before the other traffic light turns green.

Three of the longest seconds of my life.

Gobbledy runs. Furry eyebrows blow in the breeze, legs wobbling from sheer speed. He hops the curb, drops his rocks, and leaps through the air for the rock.

I snatch Gobbledy up and stuff him into Dougal's bag of candy. He grumbles until I give him the rock. He takes it in both hands and squeezes it tight.

Dougal swoops down, grabs all of the rocks from the sidewalk, and shoves them deep into his pants pockets. "We've got to get out of here before anyone recognizes us and tells Dad."

Sixteen

"Let's go to your house," Dougal says urgently to Fi.

Shaking her head, she says, "No, my sister is home. And she's nosier than your dad."

True. I run up the front steps and open the door. Dad is nowhere in sight. I hold tight to the plastic bag Gobbledy has his head sticking out of and run for the stairs. Fi and Dougal are right behind me.

Halfway up the stairs, I hear Dad yell, "Why is everyone acting so weird?"

It sounds like he's in the kitchen. I run faster.

"I got a new cat harness, Mr. D.," Fi yells back.

There is a pause, where all I hear is the sound of my own heartbeat pounding in my ears, and Gobbledy struggling to stay upright in the bag.

A second later, Dad says, "Which doesn't really explain all of this lunacy."

"Cat walking is all the rage," she yells, cresting the top of the stairs with me. Fi stops suddenly. "Hold on. I have to get my laptop. I did some research while you were gone. You're not gonna like this."

"Run interference on Dad," I say, but before I finish,

Gobbledy rips the bag open with his teeth and falls to the floor with a thud. Clutching his rock, he makes a run for the attic stairs. By the time I reach the top, I find him gently setting his rock in the Pet Rock carrier.

"Do you want to be grounded until you're old enough to vote?" Dougal yells.

"No, but—"

"He eats everything. We don't know what he is. He runs off when we're gone."

I walk over to the window to inspect. I'm pretty sure I can tie it shut with a piece of rope, but that's only a short-term solution, because I'm also sure Gobbledy can chew through the rope if he wants. Fi runs up the stairs breathlessly and flips her laptop open.

"So, there's this blog run by a group of people who look into organizations that aren't legit."

Turning the screen around so I can see it, she points at two of the biggest losers I've ever seen. They're both overweight with long, stringy hair. I wrinkle my brow and say, "They look like they've been living in a basement eating junk food for pretty much their entire lives."

"They have," Fi says, matter-of-fact. Their plump, white faces fill the screen. They're dressed in camo and holding cameras and other gear. Fi raises an eyebrow. "Meet the Planetary Society."

"What?"

Squinting at the screen, Dougal asks, "You mean they work for the Planetary Society?"

Fi inhales a moment, and then says, "No. They *are*

the Planetary Society. They run the whole thing out of their parents' basement. Most of the time they chase ghosts, but when viral videos are slim, they chase lights in the sky and aliens."

Dougal's whole face turns white. "We sent them all our information."

We all look at each other.

Finally, I break the silence. "Okay, we have to go back and get that piece of Gobbledy's craft. If we leave it there, they'll find it and take all the credit."

"Plus, they'll tell everyone," Dougal adds.

I glance over at Gobbledy sitting on the sofa, with his legs stretched out in front of him, Pet Rock carrier sitting on his lap. He looks so content.

"Dexter?"

My eyes shoot to the door. Stairs creak as Dad walks to the top.

Fi's eyes go wide, and she grabs Gobbledy so quick that his rock carrier falls to the sofa. Grabbing her laptop, she hides Gobbledy behind the screen. He grumbles.

Dad crests the top of the stairs, stepping around the corner into the attic.

We're all staring at him.

"Hey," he says nervously. "What's everyone doing up here?"

"A project," Fi says quickly.

"Oh," Dad says, his eyes stopping on Mom's village. He's quiet for a second; then he sighs. Walking over to the village, he looks down and touches the Town Hall.

Fi steps to the side, holding her laptop close, so Dad can't see around the edges.

"Mom loved this village," he says, walking his fingers down the boulevard.

We all hold our breath, waiting for him to leave.

"So," he says, turning away from the miniature town, spotting the Pet Rock carrier on the sofa. "I see you've taken a liking to your Pet Rock." Picking it up, he turns it around in his hand. "A Pet Rock is a special responsibility." He winks.

Gobbledy peeks over the screen and growls.

Dad looks up. "What was that?"

Fi pushes Gobbledy's head back down behind the screen and says, "A new app I have that plays random animal noises."

Good save.

"Huh. Okay," Dad stares at the carrier. "I love the Pet Rock. I still remember mine. Rocky. Then I got a second one and named it Adrian."

We all nod at Dad's nostalgic film moment. Gobbledy growls again. He doesn't care about Dad and his corny old movies.

"That sounds so real," Dad looks straight at Fi's laptop. "Anyway, is your sister home?"

Fi nods vigorously.

"Do you think she'd mind keeping an eye on everyone while I run back to work?"

Fi pinches her lips together and then says, "I think she'd love to, Mr. D."

"Okay, well, that's settled," Dad says, handing the Pet Rock carrier to me. "I'll be home later. We'll figure out dinner."

Dad isn't even down the stairs before Gobbledy pops his head up from behind the laptop and does a nosedive through the air, grabbing the Pet Rock carrier out of my hand.

Fi lets out the breath she's been holding and sets her laptop back on the table.

Gobbledy squeezes his milk bottle with one arm and the carrier with the other.

Dougal slaps his hands on his head and squeezes. "This is too much stress."

Fi points at the Planetary Slackers. "We have to go get that piece." She points to Gobbledy. "And you have to stay here."

He sort of waddles over to the edge of the sofa, hops to the table, and touches the computer screen.

Suddenly, it goes black. Then, a view of a strange-looking planet fills the screen. Odd and barren, no life in sight, a dying sun far in the background.

Fi and I look at each other. When I look back at the screen, Mom's face is there. She is smiling into Dad's camera in a video I remember. A field of buttercups. Mom holds Dougal in the air, spinning round and round in the sea of flowers, with late afternoon sky shining in the background. I run out to her in the video. I am, maybe, eight years old.

Dougal stares at the screen, mesmerized, and whispers, "That's Mom."

"It is," I whisper back.

Gobbledy takes his finger off the screen, and the video disappears.

Dougal leans down. "How did you do that?"

Fi looks at me, and I know exactly what she's thinking.

"I told you, there's something special about him."

I suck in a breath. "We've got to go."

"He can't stay here," Dougal argues.

"He has to stay here." I turn to Gobbledy. "If we leave you here, can you behave and stay inside?"

Gobbledy looks at all of us, then nods.

"That's not convincing," Dougal points out. "Dad could come home while we're gone."

"He just needs something to do."

Squeezing his Pet Rock carrier, Gobbledy leans back on the sofa, skinny legs stretched out, curling his eight toes on each foot.

Fi clicks around on her laptop and sets it on the sofa, pointing at the footage from the forest. "You'll be able to see us when we're in the forest, so you don't have to worry. Do you understand?"

Gobbledy locks eyes with her a second, squeezes his milk bottle, and nods.

Seventeen

Once we crest the top of the riverbank, I see the piece of metal sticking up.

"Come on," I yell, turning sideways, half sliding and half bracing myself down the muddy bank. I realize I should have changed into the pair of tennis shoes already covered in mud. Looking at the brown goo covering the tops and sides, I roll my eyes. Fi slams into me, almost knocking me into the river.

Grabbing my arm, she throws her body backwards to keep us both from falling. "Whoa. Sorry about that."

We turn our attention to the hunk of metal sticking up out of the mud. Reaching out to touch it, I feel how it's different and thin, but not like a can. Textured, but not like a metal on Earth. I grasp it firmly and pull.

A huge sucking sound erupts from the mud as the piece moves but doesn't come out.

Dougal yells from the top of the embankment. "We need a rope or shovels."

Fi leans down, digging mud with her hands. "We don't have time."

A second later, Dougal waves his hands wildly and drops to his stomach, commando-style.

"Why are you acting like a freak?"

Not only does Dougal not like dirt, he actually folds his clothes.

"Shh!"

Before I can say anything, he launches himself over the top of the embankment. "Someone's coming," he hisses.

Fi and I duck down. Footsteps thump down a path. It sounds like boots. Holding our breath, we listen to the crackle of leaves.

Pushing myself up, I peek over the top. A split second later, I push myself back down, out of sight.

"What is it?" Fi whispers.

I actually swallow back the lump in my throat. "It's the guys from the website."

"What?" Dougal's head pops up for a split second. "Oh, my god," he whispers. "Dexter's right."

Score. My big-brain little brother just said I'm right. Except he looks scared, and that worries me. I wait and listen. The sound of the river makes it hard to hear what they're saying. Fi lies on the sloped riverbank, one hand on the piece of metal, the other propped up so she can hear. Footsteps thump closer. Together, we all push further down the bank until my muddy shoes are inches from the water. The cold seeps through my jacket. We're in a bit of a time crunch. Dragging a hunk of metal into the house after Dad returns isn't an option. We really, really need to be on the move.

Fi raises up, listening.

"What?" I whisper.

"I think they're moving away from us." Popping her head up, she looks around.

"What are they doing?"

"Looking for their next viral video, as far as I can tell."

We wait.

"How can we be sure they're gone?" Dougal whispers.

"We can't," Fi says, digging mud away with her hands. "We just have to risk it. Help me."

Pushing closer, I start digging the hunk of metal out while Dougal keeps watch.

The metal moves as Fi pushes.

"How are we doing?" I whisper to Dougal.

He gives me a thumbs-up.

Fi and I rock the metal back and forth. The sides are gunmetal grey, with grooves and burn marks. With one great heave, Fi and I yank it out of the mud.

"Dougal," I whisper. "Are we clear?"

Turning around, he says, "I think so."

"Okay, climb to the top, and Fi and I will push this up to you."

Saluting, he climbs up and spins around, reaching for the metal. As he slowly pulls, it disappears over the top. Turning so Fi can use my shoulder to climb up, I say, "Give me a hand once you get up there."

I wobble with nothing to grab onto and fall backwards in the river. I'd like to say it's slow motion or like in the movies, but really, it's just fast and cold. My head sinks underwater before I surface, gasping for the breath I didn't have time to take.

"*Dexter!*" Fi yells, tumbling down the bank to give me a hand.

At the top, Dougal holds the piece of metal upright, eyes wide.

My wet clothes make it hard to flip around, but I do. As I reach for Fi's hand, she grabs hold of me and pulls. I don't know what's worse, the cold water, or the cold air. I slosh onto the muddy bank, missing one shoe and feeling like I weigh a thousand pounds.

"We're on a schedule," Dougal says, extending a hand.

It takes all three of us to carry the piece of craft. What was easy to push up the bank is ridiculously hard to carry block after block in freezing wet clothes. Dougal and Fi are on one side, me on the other. My bare foot slaps the concrete.

One of our neighbors drives by and waves. Dougal ducks behind the metal. Cutting through backyards, we head for our porch, when out of the corner of my eye I see Dad's car turn into the driveway.

"Reverse," I yell over my shoulder.

Dougal grunts. "What's going on?"

Before I have a chance to reply, Dougal sees Dad's car and immediately backs up, falling over a flower planter Mom left on the side of the garage.

"Shh . . ." I whisper, thinking fast. "I'm going to intercept Dad. When I get to the attic, I'll open the window and signal for you to bring it up."

"That almost sounds too easy," Dougal says.

Fi rolls her eyes. "All plans are easy until you have to make sure they work."

Gobbledy pops the broken window open, chattering.

My eyes shoot to Dad, sitting in his ugly brown station wagon in the driveway. Looking back up at Gobbledy, I hiss, "What are you doing?"

Chattering excitedly, he pushes the window open more and I think he's about to jump, when he hoists an empty peanut butter container out. I watch it fall to the ground and roll to a stop next to Dad's car door.

Great.

Gobbledy nods his head wildly, then lets the window fall shut.

Without wasting another second, I make a run for the back door.

Dad's car door opens.

I am on the steps, running.

Dad clears his throat. "Dexter, did you throw trash in the driveway?"

I stop, frozen, trying to think of an excuse. "Yes," I say, finally, "It rolled out of my hand."

Dad picks it up. Inhaling sharply, he says, "I see."

I have to get to the attic. My teeth are chattering.

"Where's your brother? And why are you outside when it's dark?"

Another lie. "We were at Fi's house so her sister could look after us."

Fi peeks her head around the garage, and I wave her back.

When I turn back to Dad, he's staring at me. "Son, are you all wet?"

Too cold to argue, I say, "I accidentally spilled water on myself at Fi's house."

Dad shakes his head. "I'm beginning to think you can't be left alone."

In my mind I can see the magnet with my name on it moving up the chart to Code Red. "It won't happen again."

Dad exhales loudly and makes a *humpf* noise. I think he's about to start yelling when he turns and walks inside, shaking his head.

Eighteen

My one wet shoe sloshes and squirts water from the side as I take the stairs two at a time.

The back door closes, and Dad's phone rings, muffled in his pocket. It's just the thing to keep him out of my business while I change clothes and figure out what to do. A pile of dirty clothes is stuffed in the bottom of my closet next to my tennis shoes, caked and flaked with a dull brown dirt.

Digging through my drawers, I find the one pair of pants I don't like. A pair of yellow-and-pink-plaid pants with an elastic waist. A gift from G-daddy who loves golf. I hold the pants up and stare at the bright pastel colors. I can't believe I have reached the point in my life where the world's most hideous pants are an option.

I suck in a breath and hold it, hold it, hold it—fastened!

My toes are frozen.

A gentle knock on my door startles me into finally exhaling. I open the door, but the hallway is empty. Dad is downstairs talking to someone on the phone.

A revved-up chatter gets my attention.

I look down.

Gobbledy is standing in the hall, holding his Pet Rock carrier.

"Oh, my god," I say. "You can't be down here. You're not supposed to leave the attic."

Dad yells up the stairs, "Dexter, did you say something?"

I glare at Gobbledy, pulling him into my room, "Just talking to myself," I yell back, rolling my eyes.

Gobbledy pulls something from behind his back. It's Dad's handheld Space Invaders game Mom bought him for Kissmas last year. "Wait a minute." I reach for the game. Gobbledy backs up, hiding it behind his back again.

"That is Dad's favorite gift of all time. And not only is Space Invaders his all-time favorite game, Mom bought it for him, so it's like his most prized possession of all time."

Gobbledy wrinkles his hairy brow.

"You have to give it back!"

Gobbledy backs up even more.

Dougal thunders up the stairs, his eyes going wide when he sees Gobbledy standing in the hall. "What is *he* doing down here?"

Shooing Gobbledy into the bedroom, he closes the door, arms dropping to his sides in total exasperation.

"What are you doing here?" I ask.

"Me and Fi got that thing into her basement. She sent me over here to get you and her laptop." Pointing at Gobbledy, he asks, "What is he doing out of the attic?"

I am about to tell him that Gobbledy marches to the beat of his own drum, when Dougal sees the game system. "That is Dad's game."

"You try to take it away from him."

Dougal stomps off. "You are going to get us into so much trouble."

Dad is waiting at the bottom of the stairs. "Hey, I thought we could decorate the tree."

Gobbledy wiggles in my backpack. I squirm to make it seem like the sound is coming from me.

"I see you changed clothes."

I nod my head in the direction of Fi's house. "I've got to help Fi with a project."

Dad points to the living room. "Okay, it's probably best, since I have to assemble the tree. I brought some boxes up from the basement. Maybe I'll have time to decorate tomorrow."

Nineteen

Fi's life is the same as mine in one way. She doesn't have her mom, either. What she does have is a dad who's gone most of the time, a big sister who takes care of her, and lots of free time.

"I'll order food," Fi says. "See if you can find any pizza coupons in that stack of mail."

My stomach growls. Pizza is my primary motivator.

Gobbledy thumps his foot and chirps.

"Oh, no you don't," I point at him as he stands on the counter, clutching his Pet Rock carrier. "Last time, you ate mine."

Gobbledy chirps louder and nods.

I frown. "I think you get excited about the wrong things."

"Like what?" Fi asks, cresting the top of the basement stairs.

"He's excited about eating my pizza," I say.

Fi pulls a drawer open. "Daddy leaves us a credit card in case we want to order out."

Two double cheese pizzas, one order of breadsticks, and three sodas. That's how much Daddy loves Fi.

Here is where I admit I've never actually been in Fi's basement. Technically, her dad doesn't allow kids downstairs, but since it's an emergency, Fi bends the rules.

Fi flips a light switch.

As my eyes adjust, I see a cross between a den, a fortress, and a storage room. Gadgets overflow from cardboard boxes stacked on old chairs and coffee tables. Four computer monitors are lined up on an old dining room table.

Dougal flips open a cardboard box, inspecting the contents. "Umm . . . Fi, what exactly does your dad do for a living?"

Fi helps me prop the piece of craft next to the table, and then bends down and fires up a computer. "Well, he worked for the State Department for a decade, until Mom died. Then, he started running covert ops, but don't tell anyone. It's supposed to be a secret. I accidentally read some of his emails."

"Your dad is a spy, and you never told me?"

"My dad is a handler, and you never asked." Fi winks.

Gobbledy points at the piece of craft and chatters.

"I know," Fi says, like she understands him perfectly.

He walks to the end of the table where Fi's laptop is open, and he lays one hand on the laptop screen, and one hand on the craft.

Images appear on Fi's screen, one at a time at first, then faster and faster, until millions of them flash across the screen at once.

Dougal steps back nervously. "What's he doing?"

Fi fills her cheeks with air and waits, keeping her eyes locked on Gobbledy.

"Wait a minute," she exhales slowly, letting the air out of her cheeks. "A truly advanced civilization wouldn't just have computers. They would make the craft a computer."

"What are you talking about?" I ask.

"Well, if you're traveling through deep space, then everything needs to conserve space and serve more than one function."

The images stop and the screen flickers. Gobbledy's hand drops to his side, and he stumbles to the right, bumping into the Pet Rock carrier. I grab him around the waist, holding him steady.

Suddenly, he glances at me, like he forgot I was there.

Static fills the screen.

A second later, an image of a barren planet becomes visible.

Gobbledy shakes his head and shivers, lowering himself to sit on the table.

Finally, Dougal breaks the silence. "You're saying his spaceship is the computer?"

Giving Gobbledy a worried look, she says, "That's exactly what I'm saying."

Touching his hairy shoulder, she asks quietly, "Hey, little pal, are you okay?"

He inhales and nods.

Fi points to the laptop screen. "That's where you lived, isn't it?"

Gobbledy turns to the screen and stares sadly at the barren landscape. A minute later, the camera recording the whole thing rises up, up, until the planet is far away.

Fi's finger touches the screen. "That camera was attached to the craft."

She touches Gobbledy gently. "You came a long way."

Gobbledy sighs.

"And judging by the look of that planet, you don't have anywhere to go back to."

Pinching up his whiskers, Gobbledy nods.

On screen, the light of a solar system takes shape. Another world. I blink. It's like watching TV, except it's real. So real that one of the occupants of that world, and part of his craft, are right next to me. I've always dreamed of this moment. I have. My entire life. But I thought some grown-up with a fancy job would be the one to discover it.

Not three kids standing in Fi's basement.

Fi inhales sharply, "Um, guys . . . this is big."

Dougal leans closer to the screen, eyes glued to a solar system far away. "This is huge."

Fi looks at all of us with the most serious expression I've ever seen. "No one can know about this. No one. If anyone finds out, they'll take him away and quarantine us. We'll never see him again."

Gobbledy stretches his long, skinny legs with his

huge feet out in front of him and pulls his Pet Rock carrier closer.

Dougal clears his throat. "He's not exactly easy to hide, Fiona."

"This isn't about hiding him anymore. It's about protecting him."

A door opens and closes above our heads. All of us freeze a second until Fi rolls her chair back. "Hold on, Fran's home. Let me go make something up."

Fi takes the basement steps two at a time.

Gobbledy wrestles another piece of double-cheese pizza from the box and devours it in eight bites.

Dougal takes a seat in Fi's chair and watches the video still playing. The universe. Out there. Full of dust and black holes and mystery. Stars bright as our own, huge glowing balls, illuminated like a home movie of deep space. Grainy and odd. The documented journey of a galactic traveler, currently snarfing down a breadstick as tall as him.

Shaking his head in awe and disbelief, Dougal says, "We've discovered life, Dexter. Do you know what this means?"

"That someday I might get into a good college?"

Rolling his eyes, he snorts, "It means we're not alone."

"You thought we were?"

"Not really, but ever since Mom died, I've questioned everything. Why this? Why that? Why her? Then, one day, you bring home a rock in a jar, and this happens."

"I admit, it's kind of weird."

Fi runs down the basement steps. "Okay, we've got more time. My sister is going to the mall."

Life on other planets, balanced by a quick trip to the mall. This is life on Earth.

The moon is high in the sky when we take Gobbledy home. The house is quiet. The refrigerator hums. I stop in the hall and listen for Dad upstairs. Gobbledy chirps and chatters.

"What's got you so excited?" I whisper.

He wags his furry finger in the direction of the living room. Pink and white light spills into the hall. I round the corner and see the glowing pink tree. Gobbledy's big feet thump across the floor as he runs straight for the bottom branches.

Dougal stops on the bottom step. "What's going on?"

"He likes the tree," I whisper.

Gobbledy chirps.

Dougal ignores us and tiptoes quietly up the stairs.

I sit on the sofa and yawn.

Gobbledy points and claps.

Boxes of ornaments lie open on the floor. I pick up a golden goose, slip a metal hook through the loop, and hang it from a branch.

"It's almost Kissmas," I say. "It was Mom's favorite holiday."

He climbs up into the branches and peers out.

My laugh turns into another yawn.

Long tufts of fur glow in the blinking light.

"Come on. It's been a long night." I reach into the branches, but he dodges. I frown. "Come on. I'm tired."

He grunts and narrows his eyes.

Footsteps echo in the upstairs hall, too heavy to be Dougal.

Dad yells from the top of the stairs. "Dexter, is that you?"

I shrink into the cushions of the sofa. "Yes."

"Son, it's late. What are you doing?"

Total lie. "It's a surprise."

Dad sighs. "You know how I feel about surprises. Have you seen my Space Invaders game?"

Ouch. "No."

Dad walks off down the hall. "Stay in bed like your brother."

Sensing danger, Gobbledy walks over and lets me pick him up. I stuff him and his carrier down into my backpack and tiptoe up the stairs. In my room, I find the empty milk bottle and hand it over. Gobbledy hugs it tight as I tuck him into an open drawer. He snuggles deep down into my clothes with his milk bottle and Pet Rock carrier. I climb in bed, too tired to take him up to the attic.

Within seconds I'm out to the world. This world, at least.

Twenty

When the door opens, I sit straight up in bed and toss my pillow over the drawer. Gobbledy makes an oomph sound but doesn't move. Dad stands in the doorway, hands at his sides, mouth open, like he's just seen the most incredible thing in the world. Tears run down his cheeks.

Dougal launches himself upright in bed. "*Wha?* Huh?"

Dad looks at both of us. Just when I think he's about to tell us we've won a raffle or a million dollars or he's putting my behavior chart in the trash, his jaw drops open, then closes.

"Dad?" I ask, quietly.

The sound of my voice makes him cry harder. "I'll be downstairs," he whispers and closes the door.

Dougal waits until he's gone. "That can't be good."

I am about to snatch the pillow off Gobbledy when Dad opens the door again. "Thank you, boys. I made hot chocolate."

A second later he's gone again.

Dougal looks at me, raising his eyebrow. "That wor-

ries me, because it is a totally unrelated response to anything that might actually be going on in this household."

Gobbledy smooths fur back off his forehead, pushing the pillow away.

I lean over and whisper, "Stay here. I have to go see
what's going on."

Gobbledy fusses with his carrier and milk bottle,
tucking them in tight. Closing his eyes, he pulls the
blanket up, rolls over, snuggles deep into his drawer
bed, and falls back to sleep.

Dougal swings his legs over the edge of the bed.
"What do you think this is about?"

"I have no idea," I say, which is the most truthful
thing I've said in a while.

Down in the living room, lights twinkle. Ornaments and
tinsel hang on the tree. The pink, sparkling spectacle is
totally magical. The tree isn't even the best part. The
best part is an entire Christmas village made from cardboard, modeling clay, Legos, dried flowers, plants, and a
string of white, sparkling lights placed down the center.

Dougal and I stand shoulder to shoulder in the doorway, mouths open.

Dad puts his arms around us. "You are both so tal-
ented."

Dougal nods. "Uh-huh."

Turning to him, Dad says, "I hope you grow up to be

an engineer. You have such skill. Mom was building that village upstairs, and now you two have done this." He steps into the living room and picks up a hand-carved decorative gourd that looks like a small house inside a cave. "This," he says, "is amazing."

I raise an eyebrow. *My thoughts exactly.*

Dougal gives me the stink eye. We are thinking the same thing. Gobbledy must have come down here in the middle of the night. It's the only explanation, other than Santa, who isn't due yet. Still, Gobbledy is pretty small, and the modeling clay and Legos are kept in the attic. Which, I suppose, is why he's currently upstairs, passed out.

Dad bursts into tears again.

It makes me nervous. I like to think the adults in my life have it all together, a belief that is shaken when he falls apart. And that makes me nervous, because plenty of stuff has been falling apart. I don't need my dad to be one of those things.

"Dad?" Dougal steps forward. "What's going on?"

Through tears and snot, Dad heaves words up from his chest, like every breath will be his last. "You've made this so special. Your mother loved the holidays. I've just dreaded this time for months, and now you two have come together to make this first Kissmas without her bearable."

Dougal looks at me and frowns.

"I'm sorry for yelling at you last night. I didn't know you were down here building a surprise. I feel like I'm always yelling at you. I'm just scared I'm not doing the right thing."

"We miss her too," I say quietly.

Slumping forward, Dad pulls me in for a big hug.

"She would have loved these decorations," Dougal says.

Dad cries harder. "We're going to see her today," he chokes in between sobs. "It's been exactly six months."

In the days after she died, I didn't know how I could get through a single day without her funny notes in my lunch. Now, I don't know if I can stand seeing her in the ground. Seeing her name carved on that tombstone makes it final. Every time I see it, chills run up my arms and legs. Most kids get the luxury of a hamster dying. Not Fi and me.

"Come on," Dad says, wiping his nose with the back of his hand. "Let's drink our hot chocolate and buy Mom some flowers."

Hot chocolate and flowers feel like a knife in the heart.

"Do you really need your backpack?" Dad asks, standing at the front door. He's washed his face and combed his hair, but his clothes are wrinkled, and he looks like a train wreck.

I nod.

Furrowing his brow, he says, "I worry about you."

Dougal steps up, "Dexter is prepared."

Not exactly the truth.

I didn't match my socks and just realized my shirt is on inside out.

Dad buys Mom the biggest, prettiest bouquet he can find at the grocery store. Dougal and I wait in the station wagon, with Gobbledy wiggling in my backpack.

I am okay with how the day is going until Dad kisses the headstone.

I don't know what to say. If Dad had actually let me have a hamster, then I'd have some practice with grief. Instead, I just stand there praying it isn't real. I am just so mad at him. All he's done is yell at me and tell me that I can't have any living creature to keep me company. I am so mad I want to explode. Until I start crying.

I can't help it. Losing someone you love is bad enough, but then having to visit the big mound of dirt they call home is just depressing.

I can't help it, and I can't stop.

Gobbledy squirms. I know he's probably worried.

Dad lays his hand on my shoulder. "Why don't you walk around and get some fresh air? I'm going to talk to Mom."

Dougal takes my hand and pulls me off in the direction of huge stone crosses. Cemeteries are full of people I will never know.

When we're far enough away but can still see Dad, I sit down and unzip the top of my pack. Gobbledy pops his head out and looks around. Dougal sits across from me on the grass.

Chattering, Gobbledy climbs out of my pack.

"You can't wander off. We'll be leaving soon."

He points to my face.

"I'm okay," I say. "I'm just sad, and kind of angry."

Rows of headstones roll away from us in every direction. I keep my eye on Dad.

Gobbledy trudges through the thick grass. He walks to a headstone and touches it cautiously.

"When you die on this planet," Dougal whispers, "they bury you in the ground."

Gobbledy turns to face him, brow furrowed.

"Do you understand?" Dougal asks.

Pointing at the ground, Gobbledy nods.

Lying down on the grass, Dougal closes his eyes like he's going to sleep. Only then do I realize he's mimicking someone dying, and I pull him upright.

Gobbledy twists his whiskers into a frown.

"I'm just trying to explain the concept," Dougal says.

"The concept sucks."

"Our mom is here," I blurt out.

Gobbledy rubs the grass with his soft, furry hand.

A hawk flies low overhead, casting a shadow on the ground. He glances up and makes a run for my backpack.

"It's okay," I say. "You're safe with us."

"That village he made in the living room is where he used to live," Dougal says, matter-of-fact.

Gobbledy's skinny legs wobble as he takes shelter in the pack, hugging his rock carrier and milk bottle.

"How do you know?"

"Trust me, I know. You build replicas of places and things you love, that are important to you. Places you want to remember. That's what Mom was doing with her village. She loved where we live."

I think about the bizarre trees, the long, crooked branches. "Those are the weirdest trees I've ever seen."

Dougal pushes up from the grass, dusting his jeans off. "They're not trees."

"What are they?"

Shaking his head, he says, "I'm not sure, but they aren't trees."

Twenty-One

Sir Shreds-A-Lot sits in the middle of our driveway.

Dad honks the horn.

The cat stares at us.

After the third honk, when the persnickety feline refuses to move and Fi doesn't come outside, Dad parks his ugly brown station wagon in the street. The Imperial March starts up in his pocket. Work is calling.

Dad sighs super loud and groans. "I have to take this call."

Dougal and I get out. I've been clutching my backpack all the way home. I unzipped the top a little so Gobbledy could get some air.

Sir Shreds walks over, circling like a shark, catching a whiff of my backpack.

"Go away," I whisper, shooing him off.

Shreds stops and yowls.

"You're kind of a butthole," I hiss.

The cat flicks his tail.

The door to the station wagon creaks open behind me. Dad clears his throat. "Hey, I've got to go put out a few ketchup fires. Do you think Fran is home?"

"Her car is gone," Dougal observes, "but she'll probably be home soon."

Dad looks around in that nervous way he does when he has to leave us alone. "Okay. I'll pick up dinner. Go inside and lock the door. Don't leave the house. Got it?"

Fran's Festiva whips into the driveway next door, jerking to a stop. Fi waves from the passenger seat.

"Hey, Mr. D.," Fran says, popping her gum.

"Oh, good," Dad says, "you're home. This is really awesome timing."

Digging his wallet out, he pulls out a bunch of ones and fives, folded together. Embarrassed by his disorganization, he hands over the wad of cash.

Fran holds up a hand with purple-tipped fingernails. "It's all good, Mr. D. I'll keep an eye on them."

Dad blushes and stuffs the money back in his pocket.

Shreds howls like someone is stepping on his tail.

Dad drives off, smoke backfiring from the tailpipe.

Dougal stares at the burst of smoke lingering in the still, cool air. "We need to get Dad a new job for Kissmas."

Fi snatches up her deranged cat. "I came over earlier, and your dad was over the moon happy. Then he burst into tears. Is he all right?"

I sigh, because I hate saying it out loud. "We went to see Mom."

Fran's whole face pinches into a frown. "Sorry. That sucks."

We all nod, especially Fi, who leans back in Fran's Festiva to grab her laptop.

Gobbledy squirms in my pack. "I need to get something to eat," I say.

"Yeah, me too," Fran agrees, "and I've got a paper due. Stay out of trouble."

"Come on," I say to Fi, "follow me."

At the doorway to the living room, I stop and point.

As soon as she sees the Christmas village her mouth drops open. "Whoa. Did Dougal build this?"

Dougal clears his throat behind us. "Nope."

Fi wanders the room, staring at the carved gourds and Lego village with the strange trees. "This is amazing. This is proof of advanced intelligence."

"Come on," I say. "I'm going to introduce the advanced life form to microwave pancakes. We skipped breakfast."

In the kitchen, I look inside my backpack. It's empty. "Has anyone seen Gobbledy?"

Dougal stands in front of the open freezer. "Nope."

Gobbledy and the Pet Rock carrier are gone.

We search the entire house, top to bottom. No Gobbledy. Not even a clue.

"What if he got out at the cemetery?" Dougal asks.

"Don't say that," I counter. "Terrible thought. Do you know how far the cemetery is? It would take us all day to walk."

"Have you seen him since we got home?"

"No, but I felt him wiggling around in my backpack."

Fi stares at her laptop screen with the saddest look in her eyes. "Come on," she says. "I know where he is."

The afternoon light is just beginning to slant across the treetops as we crest the hill leading to the playground. The woods glow. We charge down the hill together.

By the time we find Gobbledy, he has buried twenty-eight rocks. Only five are left.

Fi runs to him. Gobbledy is covered in dirt and shaking from the cold.

"He's burying them," Dougal whispers.

Twenty-eight tiny graves.

It's terrible. Worse than terrible.

"Come on," Fi says, dropping to her knees. "We have to help."

Because winter hasn't really set in, we can still dig with our hands. We have five holes in no time.

Carefully, Gobbledy lifts each rock, lowering it into a hole. Using his hands, he covers the rock with dirt, then moves on to the next one.

Dougal starts crying. "This is sad."

I put my hands on my hips and stare at the thirty-three graves that represent the rest of his people. They came so far. When Mom died, I thought I could will her back to life. Now, here he is, burying everyone he knew on this strange planet they managed to crash-land on. Everything feels so hopeless. I sit down on the ground. A second later, everyone joins me.

Gobbledy picks up twigs, and acorns, big colorful leaves, and lays them on top of the graves. The day's final rays stream down through the branches. The forest is quiet, except for the sound of the river. The rush of water and snap of twigs, as we watch our friend say good-bye.

The only other rock left glows and hums in the carrier.

Twenty-Two

On Monday, my science teacher, Mr. Rodriguez, looks up from his notebook and says, "Okay Dexter, this is the absolute final day to turn in your science project."

My entire body seizes up.

My project.

Cricket Colony.

The habitat I totally forgot to repopulate because I've been chasing around a rock from another star system. The project I abandoned after Gobbledy sprouted in a jar. A big lump lodges in my throat. Maybe I'll pass out, and my teacher will be so concerned with keeping me alive, he'll forget that I don't have my project.

Mr. Rodriguez smiles at me. "I know that to some of you, science is a way of life, and you've been working on your projects a long time. I am eager to see the results."

An F in science means no trip to the island off the coast of Georgia to see G-mama and G-daddy.

An F in science means grounding, which is going to be a big problem, since I keep having to go back and forth to the forest.

An F in science is whatever is beyond Code Red, which I promised to avoid.

F does not stand for fun.

An F in science is pretty much the end of the world.

In a moment of utter desperation, I blurt out, "I forgot my project." I nod my head furiously, thinking this might help me irrationally conjure a project out of thin air.

My left eye starts to twitch.

My science teacher cocks his head. "You?"

Someone save me.

"It has to be turned in today," he says, walking down the aisle.

Help!

SOS!

My brain howls.

Code Red! Code Red!

I forgot all about this project since I hatched Gobbledy.

I can't turn him in.

No way.

But. . . .

Maybe I could turn in the rock. It has a nice carrier.

My science teacher stops at the blackboard. "This project counts for one third of your grade."

He locks eyes with me, and my skin starts to itch.

Help.

Where can I find a science project in thirty seconds or less?

My eye twitches.

My brain buzzes.

Code Red! Code Red!

My science teacher clears his throat. "Where is your project, Dexter?"

Massive lie on the way. As soon as I think of one. "At home."

"Can you call your father and have him drop it off at the office?"

If I nod, the questions will stop.

Nod. I want to nod.

I can't nod.

I shake my head. *Code Red! Code Red!*

Mr. Rodriguez does not look happy.

I change my answer and shrug, "Maybe."

He taps his finger on the board, then points to the door. "Step into the hall, please."

My heart beats so fast I can't breathe. I stand on wobbly knees and follow him into the hall. He closes the door so we can be alone. Not a good sign.

No science project.

Bad grade.

Parent–teacher conference.

Alien living in the attic.

The four walls of my bedroom closing in on me forever.

Aargh!

"Dexter?"

I look up at my science teacher. "Huh?"

"I want you to tell me the truth. Do you have a project you've been working on? You said you did."

I nod.

I nod vigorously. Because, really, what am I supposed to do?

Gobbledy is *quite* the project.

I am currently studying advanced forms of life and how they adapt to a new planet.

"And will you be turning this project in today?"

My eyes scan the hall for clues.

"Dexter?"

My eyes settle on a pebble from the playground near someone's locker.

I have a set of crystals I've been growing. No log or notes, but maybe I can throw something together.

"Dexter?"

"Yes. I have my project."

Lies.

Massive lies.

He cocks his head and raises his eyebrow, the way he does when he doesn't believe you.

"Look," I say, diving in for the big save. "I just have to finish a few notes. And well—I've got to go home and get it." I drop my eyes to the floor in an effort to appear more innocent. "If that's okay."

Down the hall, a rowdy group of kids rounds the corner on their way to recess. I see Dougal in the sea of faces. He looks at my science teacher, then at me, and frowns.

I give him a big thumbs-up, but it just makes him suspicious. He slows to a stop and peeks back around the corner.

Laying his hand on my shoulder, my science teacher says, "Okay. You're one of my favorite students. I'll write you a pass to go home and get your project. Have it in by the end of the day."

He opens the door to the classroom.

Whew.

Disaster averted.

That was close.

Mr. Rodriguez hands me a pass.

I grab my backpack and go.

My super nosy little brother is still peering around the corner, spying. I run for the backdoor.

Dougal breaks into a run, hissing, "What's going on with you today?"

"I forgot to turn in a project. That's all."

"Why did you just get called into the hall?"

"I was—there was a mix-up." I run faster, rounding a corner. The huge double doors come into view.

"Humph," he says, "I don't believe you."

I shrug. Not the first time.

Shifting my backpack, I yell, "I have to go."

"You never fixed the Cricket Colony. You don't have anything to turn in."

I come to a complete stop and turn around. "If you actually noticed that I'd forgotten my project, then why didn't you say something?"

His eyes get bigger. "I just remembered when I saw you standing in the hall. So, what are you going to turn in?"

I shrug and glance up at the ceiling, trying to avoid answering.

"I'll give you my project."

"You don't have a project."

"I've been working on the moons of Jupiter in my spare time."

"That's cheating." Though I can justify it if I really try. In a total emergency.

Like a major crisis. And this is becoming a major crisis.

"Think of it as borrowing."

I groan. I hate logic.

Dougal glances up at the clock in the hall. "Come on. We have to go. The bell is about to ring."

Twenty-Three

Gobbledy drags his rock carrier into the lab, chattering softly, excited to see us.

Dougal groans. "I thought you were taking the moons."

My eyes scan the wooden table. Real moss experiment. Crystal growing. Or buy more crickets. These are really my only choices. Moss, crystals, crickets. I'll have to make up some notes, but it's better than cheating. I forgot, but I can still bring in a fair grade. A decent grade.

A car stops out front. A second later, car doors slam shut. Dad is supposed to be at work. How can this be happening? I run to the living room to check. Gobbledy growls, low and menacing.

Behind me, Dougal mutters. "That little monster growled at me."

"It's the only rock he has left. He's being protective."

On the other side of the window, I hear footsteps in the driveway. My heart skips a beat. I duck down from the window.

"Dexter," Dougal yells. "He's developing some sort of aggressive posture with me."

I jerk my head up and peer out the window. Two men stand in our driveway. They're both dressed all in black, but I can see their faces.

It's the two guys from the Planetary Society.

I crawl across the living room on my stomach, commando style. When I roll into the hallway, I see Dougal glaring at me from the other end.

He opens his mouth and I hiss, "Shh."

Lowering his voice, he asks, "Why are you acting like such a freak?"

Gobbledy squeezes his Pet Rock carrier and says, "Shh."

Dougal rolls his eyes. "Why are you on the floor whispering?"

I jerk my thumb toward the front door. "Those two goons from the Planetary Society are out front."

Dougal narrows his eyes. "What? How do you know?"

"In an attempt to seem legit, they're wearing Planetary Society T-shirts. It's kind of hard to miss."

Dougal covers his mouth with his hand. "They traced Fi's number."

I wince. "Maybe."

Dougal runs quick and light to the living room. "Not maybe. Definitely."

Footsteps thump across the front porch. Dougal stops mid-stride, eyes wide. I whip my head around. Sensing danger, Gobbledy wraps his arms around his carrier and backs up into my lab.

Shoes scuffle against the porch. I hold my breath and listen.

Dougal and I look at each other.

The doorknob jiggles.

Dougal leans forward and whispers, "We left the backdoor unlocked."

Without a second to waste, he launches himself up and sprints down the hall into the kitchen. A second later I hear the lock click.

Gobbledy pushes the door to my lab closed.

Dougal peeks around the corner. I wave him down the hall. One of the goons tries to peek through the living room window. I step completely out of sight.

D-man stops and listens.

I point to my lab.

He nods.

I look over my shoulder, make sure the coast is clear, and run. I skid to a stop, push my lab door open, and close it quickly behind Dougal. Footsteps thump up the back-porch steps. It's dark and quiet, except for the golden glow of the rock, and our breathing.

Gobbledy chitters anxiously.

The knob on the backdoor jiggles.

My whole body tenses. "Why are they trying to get into our house?" I whisper.

There's just enough light from the bottom of the door to see Dougal tilt his head in Gobbledy's direction. "They want our friend."

The front door opens, and slams shut.

My jaw drops. "How did they get in?"

Dougal covers his face with his hands. "We're gonna die."

"We are not going to die," I growl.

Though, at the moment, there is no evidence to back up such a claim.

Footsteps stomp down the hall and into the kitchen. I hold my breath. Gobbledy squeezes his carrier so tight the cardboard crinkles. We have to hide him. The footsteps start back down the hall. Dougal squeezes the doorknob, in case one of the goons tries to open it.

Slowly and soundlessly, I open my backpack and tap Gobbledy on the shoulder. I tilt it so he can climb inside with the carrier and his milk bottle.

Footsteps thump up the stairs. Gobbledy inhales long and deep before I zip the top shut.

"Let's make a run for it," Dougal says softly.

The thought occurred to me, but I was worried. "We don't know where the other one is."

"Huh?"

"There's two goons. One is upstairs. What if the other one is in the hall waiting?"

"Right. Good point."

In the middle of a crisis, my little brother just admitted I'm right. Score.

The footsteps stop at the top of the stairs. Dougal's hand squeezes the doorknob tight. Silently, I hook the straps of my backpack through my arms and snap the wrap-around belt for support.

I whisper over my shoulder. "Gobbledy? Are you okay?"

He signals with a low chirp.

"Dexter?" A voice yells from upstairs.

Dougal covers his face with his hands. "They know your name. We're doomed."

"Dougal?" The voice yells.

We look at each other.

Dad!

I throw open the door and run into the hall. Dad stands at the top of the staircase.

"What in the world are you doing, Son? Where is your brother?"

"In my secret lab," I say hesitantly, wary of the question-and-answer game. Answers are often wrong. Wrong answers lead straight to Code Red.

Dad frowns so tight he might explode. "The school called and said Dougal disappeared."

My little brother gasps behind me. "Oh, no. He's right. I left before the final bell."

Angry Dad takes the stairs two at a time. "What is going on?" Angry Dad is not happy. In all my years on Earth, I've never seen that look. The confusion, the frustration, the anger . . . well, okay, maybe I have seen that look before. "I forgot my science project."

"So, you kidnapped your little brother?"

D-man steps out of the lab. "I came along to help."

Dad squeezes the banister tight, like he's going to rip it off and shred it with his teeth. "You need two people to get the one thing you weren't supposed to forget in the first place?"

Logic and reason do not work with adults. I pull a tight smile and say, "Get the crystals, D-man."

Behind me, Dougal snaps his fingers and yells, "Right." He runs into my lab where he shuffles jars, trying to sound busy.

Dad walks down the hall, stopping in between us. He jams his hands deep in his Ketchup Factory jacket. "I want you to know that I don't believe a word of this."

I want to huff loud and long, but Dad's brow is pinched extra tight, so I give it to him straight. "I told you. I forgot my project. It's due today. Mr. Rodriguez wrote me a note to come home and get it. It counts for a third of my grade."

"Eureka!" Dougal shrieks. "Crystals." He steps quickly into the hall clutching my Crystal City.

Angry Dad eyes Dougal. "So, do you want to explain why the school is calling about you now? In the middle of a new round of layoffs at work. You? The good son?"

"Umm." My little brother clears his throat, "I'm sorry, Dad. I saw Dexter in the hall and lost my mind."

Angry Dad looks at me, then back at Dougal. "It's easy to lose your mind when your brother is involved." Dad looks at his watch, "So what time is your project officially due?"

"Last bell," I say, suddenly realizing we've spent a lot of time hiding from the . . . "Did you happen to see anyone outside?" I ask.

"Like who?"

Dougal catches on fast. "Like people who look like they're from a Planetary Society?"

Dad cocks his head. "Son, you've managed to not be crazy. Don't start now. We have exactly seven minutes to get to school and turn that project in on time. Then you'll have to go to work with me. You obviously can't be left alone."

Twenty-Four

At the curb, in front of the main building, the station wagon jerks to a stop and stalls, backfiring. Snarly Watson crosses the courtyard carrying a large stack of costumes. The noise gets her attention. She yells, "Dress rehearsal." Squinting in my direction, she jerks her bony finger toward the auditorium.

Dad groans inside the station wagon. "What does that mean?"

I shrug. "I don't know, exactly."

"Hurry up. I have to get back to work, Son. I've got a surprise corporate inspection. I've got brown ketchup and layoffs, and you're making me nuts."

I unzip my backpack slowly. Gobbledy looks up. I shake my head, and he puts his furry finger to his lips. Carefully I trade with Dougal, handing over my pack and taking Crystal City.

I jump out of the station wagon and run, sliding to a stop in front of the science room.

Mr. Rodriguez pushes his chair under his desk. "Dexter," he smiles. "I was beginning to think this was a bust."

"No way." I walk into the classroom and set Crystal City on an empty desk.

He inspects it from all sides. "This is a very cool structure you've got here. Did you put this together all by yourself?"

I nod. "I grew all the crystals and tried to shape them into something resembling a city."

"This is an incredible project. I love all the special touches you've added to the completely natural setting."

Compliments often lead to passing grades.

"Okay," he says, "I'll grade these over break."

🎁

The backstage light is dim. Snarly Watson is on the other side of the curtain, calling names.

"Jason Roebucks?"

Tennis shoes squeak across the stage. There's a pause.

"Dexter Duckworth," she huffs out loud.

A cold reality seizes me. I am going to have to perform in this ridiculous, embarrassing extravaganza.

She yells, big and loud and annoyed, "*Dexter!*"

I lift up the bottom of the curtain and pop onto the stage. The entire cast turns to stare at me.

Snarly Watson huffs and thrusts a shimmering, satiny, gold thing at me. "This is your costume. Protect it with your life."

My classmates are dutifully lined up across the

stage. A nervous twitch pinches the edges of their mouths, except for Jason Roebucks, who is so happy to be playing the Snow King that it scares the Snow Queen. Roebucks comes from one of those families that think landing the lead in the fifth-grade Winter Extravaganza means he's gifted. All he has to do is hold a fake staff with a crystal ball on the end and put his arm around his pretend wife. Miss Watson clutches a plastic snowman by one arm, swinging it here and there, so as to better make her point.

The snowman slaps against her thigh. She growls, "Does everyone know their lines?"

The cast nods, obediently. I shake my head. I don't know any of my lines. They are written in a script I've ignored in my backpack. The one I plan to throw away or shred or lose or launch to the moon.

Miss Watson points the snowman at us. "Is everyone excited for the Winter Extravaganza?"

Embarrassed. Embarrassed is the word she's looking for.

Jason Roebucks thrusts his arm high in the air. "My mom made me a special belt out of silk. Is it okay to wear it?"

Miss Watson beams at his initiative. "Yes," she says. Then, she turns abruptly to the Candy Cane Chorus.

The eyes of the snowman reflect stage light, glinting wildly. "Does everyone know their cues?" She glares at me.

More nods. I frown, shaking my head. She ignores me.

"Okay," she continues. "I'll be right here in the wings. I will guide you through this production with every fiber of my being." She swings the snowman so high and with such force that his arm comes off in her hands. The plastic body sails to the stage floor. A hideous sight. A one-armed snowman with a dent in his white belly.

The Snow Queen reaches for the doll, but Miss Watson snatches it up quick.

"A reporter from the *Daily Times* will be here to re-view the play, so put on a happy face." Her lips curl around her crooked tooth as she jams the arm back into the socket and hands it to the king and queen. "You're dismissed."

Twenty-Five

The Ketchup Factory is all out of holiday cheer. Limp tinsel hangs from an old, plastic tree spray-painted white. Faded red balls sag on metal hooks. Lights hang from metal ceiling pipes, cords straining to reach the plug. At the very top of the tree, an angel leans precariously to one side. Flecks of white paint dot the floor, where not a single present is under the tree.

Gobbledy chirps in my backpack.

Dougal makes a sharp right turn into the break room and cuts his eyes at me. "We may never be able to go home again. I can't believe you did this."

"Stop blaming me."

I set my backpack on a plastic table and unzip the top. Gobbledy pops his head out, taking long breaths, looking around at the room.

Dougal digs around in his pockets for change. When he's collected a handful, he walks over to the vending machine. He pops four coins into the slot, presses a few buttons, and a bag of Cheesy Twisters tumbles over the edge.

Gobbledy claps his hands and smacks his lips.

Dougal groans. "Who knows what those lunatics are planning."

Squire Roberts rounds the corner carrying a tray of fresh, hot French fries.

Gobbledy lowers himself down into my pack, out of sight, grumbling.

Squire sets the tray on the table. Fresh, hot French fries lure Gobbledy out of hiding. He stretches his little arm out, reaching for a fry. I intercept and push him back in my pack.

Dougal snatches the bag out of the vending machine tray and rips it open with his teeth.

Squire dusts off his hands and announces, "So, we're going to do some taste testing while your father is in meetings. Word has it that corporate suits are on their way, and I am entrusted with the task of keeping you out of the way."

Dougal hands me the bag of Cheesy Twisters. "Don't you have to use the bathroom?"

I have no idea what he's talking about. "Huh?"

Dougal jerks his eyes to my backpack, where a little furry arm is stretched out trying to snatch a carton of fries from the tray.

Leaning in close, D-man whispers, "You have to get him out of here. The French fries are going to make him lose his mind."

If I had traveled all the way across the galaxy, I'd probably really love Earth food too. Pizza, sub sandwiches, cheese dip. I sigh, thrust a bunch of fries into

Gobbledy's hand, and shove the bag of Cheesy Twisters into my backpack.

Squire opens a drawer and pulls out hair protectors and gloves. He hands me and Dougal one of each.

Gobbledy chomps warm, delicious fries.

"I really do have to use the bathroom," I say, hoisting up my backpack.

Dougal puts on the hair protector, which poofs up like a big shower cap.

Squire grabs a sleeve of saltine crackers. "All right," he says to us. "First, we clear our palate with a saltine. Then, we swish some water around in our mouth. Then we are ready to taste, record scores, clear our palate, and start again. Got that Dex?"

I nod.

"And wash those hands," Squire reminds me.

I frown. First of all, I'm not really going to the bathroom. Second of all, I am old enough to know I have to wash my hands. I put the hair protector on and walk into the hallway. Inside my pack, Gobbledy chatters, not happy about being separated from the French fries.

I walk forever, trying to find the bathroom. Each hall leads to a longer maze. Deep in the corridors, the roar of ketchup production is reduced to a low rumble. I am just about to round a corner when I hear a factory worker ask, "Can I help you?"

A man says, "We're here on business."

I stop and listen.

Gobbledy's head pops out of my pack, and he growls.

The factory worker pauses a second. "Oh, yeah. You guys must be from corporate, to run the tests and do the inspection."

"Yes," the man answers.

I creep over and peek around the corner.

The factory worker asks, "Do you want me to show you to the lab?"

"We know the way," the Planetary Goon says. They're wearing stolen lab coats over their T-shirts. "We are looking for a boy. Have you seen him?"

I back up. *It's the men from the driveway. Run. Run now.*

I head for the nearest door and yank it open. Concrete stairs climb upward as far as my eyes can see. I close the door carefully, not making a sound. Then I run. The stairs spiral up in a never-ending maze. Judging by the number of floors, I have to be approaching the roof. Out of breath and sweating heavily, I round the corner of the final landing.

"Gobbledy? Are you okay?"

A chattering, ticking sound emanates from my backpack. I take that as a yes. I reach for a big metal door. I hear voices in the stairwell below.

Speaking in Goon.

Yikes.

Quickly, I pull the door open. It leads to an empty corridor. Okay, if I go right, it takes me back toward the main office. *Right?* I try to focus. Left goes to the production area. *Maybe.*

Footsteps echo up the stairwell.

I adjust my pack and take off running. Halls lead to more halls. Just when I am about to give up hope, I round a corner and run smack into a door marked: RESTRICTED. EMPLOYEES ONLY.

Twenty-Six

I've never been so relieved to see a restricted area in all my life. The bag of Cheesy Twisters crinkles in my backpack. The occupant is antsy. I push the big metal door open. The roar of machinery is loud. The door slams shut behind us. I reach back to check the hall, but the door cannot be opened from this side. Gobbledy bumps and thumps. I pull my backpack off, and Gobbledy pops up, clutching his Pet Rock carrier with one hand and Cheesy Twisters with the other. After a second, he clamps his hands over his ears and screams.

"It's okay," I say. I pick up my pack and walk fast. He looks up at my face. I touch the soft fur on his skinny shoulders. "It's okay," I promise. "I will get us out of here."

More importantly, we have to stay on the move. I adjust my protective hair covering and step out onto a catwalk.

Heavy machinery rattles and hums. It's like being in the belly of a beast. I walk out on the metal grating and look straight down. Several floors below, ketchup churns in big vats the size of my backyard. The view is great, except my stomach is doing somersaults because I am so high up. Catwalks stretch the entire length of the production floor. Clean, shiny tomatoes roll down conveyor belts. Thick, red ketchup gurgles and roils in vats.

Gobbledy pops his head out of my pack. He glances furtively across the catwalks, presses his hands to his ears, and screams again. I try to pull him out of my pack, but he clutches the carrier tight. I kneel down fast.

I yell over the noise, "We've got to hide. Those guys are chasing us again."

Gobbledy looks back at the door frantically.

"We'll be okay," I yell, certain I just told a huge lie. "Just stay calm."

His eyes sweep over the ketchup vats. Then he does something no one should ever do.

He looks down.

His eyes swell to the size of small moons. He shoots straight up, knocking his carrier onto the catwalk. Using my ninja reflex, I snatch him in mid-air and hold tight. I see the carrier out of the corner of my eye, but it takes a second to realize what's happening as it tumbles to the edge of the catwalk. It hovers a single second, before falling over the edge. To my utter horror, I watch it fall *down, down, down,* where it smacks into a vat of red goo. Floating and bobbing, it sails in a sea of ketchup.

That's problem number one.

Problem number two becomes a firm reality when Gobbledy realizes his rock is gone. Before I can squeeze him tight, he launches himself out of my grip into a wobbly swan dive. I lean over the railing and watch as he smacks the surface of the ketchup and goes under.

Against all logic, I grab my hair protector and scream. "Gobbledy! What are you doing?"

It's a dumb question. I can see what he's doing. Gobbledy is swimming in ketchup while goons chase us. My eyes dart in every direction. The ketchup workers are in a company-wide meeting. Each vat is at least thirty feet high. At the end of the catwalk, a spiral staircase winds down to the production floor. I hoist my backpack onto my shoulder and run for the stairs. Round and round I run, watching Gobbledy bob in globs of ketchup, now clutching his Pet Rock carrier. I jump down the last few steps, run speedy fast to a big metal ladder attached to the vat, and throw my pack on the concrete floor. Cresting the top, I see Gobbledy on the other side. A single bubble of ketchup rises to the surface and blurps.

"Gobbledy," I scream over the noise, "Swim. The ketchup is heating up."

There aren't many things worse than being boiled alive in a vat of ketchup. Maybe a few, but I don't want to think about that at the moment.

Gobbledy positions his carrier in front of him and pushes, kicking his legs.

Across the production floor, a big, metal door opens. The two goons walk in. One carries a piece of rope and a camera. The other, a canvas bag.

I duck fast.

The roar of machinery is loud enough to hide Gobbledy's grunts, but my backpack is a problem. I climb down to the bottom, snatch my pack up with one hand, and within seconds I am at the top of the ladder again. Gobbledy struggles in the middle. The big vat churns ketchup, creating a sort of whirlpool. Another bubble blurps to the surface. Over the top of the vat, I see the goons headed our way.

There's just enough space on the ladder to hook my pack so it hangs above the ketchup. Carefully, with my eyes on the goons, I climb over the top. After hooking my pack, I sink down into the warm, gooey ketchup. Below me, the goons round the corner. I duck. Gobbledy swims harder. I tread ketchup, but it's thick. I push off the metal side and launch myself into the center. With a renewed sense of hope, Gobbledy pushes his carrier toward me. More bubbles blurp to the surface. The warm, squishy sauce heats up fast. I stretch my arm as far as it will go, and grab Gobbledy's hand. The big, metal doors leading to the main hallway clank shut.

Please let that be the sound of two disgruntled Planetary Goons leaving the building empty-handed.

Twenty-Seven

The women's bathroom is the best option. Here's my thinking on the matter: if someone walks in and catches me washing ketchup out of my armpits, it will definitely not be my dad. And that is a good thing. Ketchup squishes out of my tennis shoes. Behind me, a trail of red footprints leads to the door. Gobbledy licks his furry hand and smacks his lips. I rinse the cardboard carrier off, and set it on the tile floor, limp, but still intact. Gobbledy is next. I position him in the sink and turn on the warm water. I pump soap on my hands and smooth it on his fur. Red water flows down the drain like blood in a horror movie. I look in the mirror and try not to panic. From the neck down, I am covered in condiment. Gobbledy scrubs ketchup clumps from his fur, since he is small enough to shower comfortably in a sink. I, on the other hand, am faced with two water supplies: sink or toilet.

"You are trouble," I hiss.

Gobbledy cocks his head and rubs his armpit.

"What were you thinking?"

He furrows his brow and clucks loudly at me. Clearly, he is saying something, I just don't know what. I unzip my backpack, hoping for a miracle. *And there it is.* The most dreaded thing on Earth is suddenly the answer to all my problems: a gingerbread man costume.

I dump my ketchup-stained shirt and pants in the trash. Standing in my underwear, I wipe the rest of the ketchup off with paper towels. I wash my tennis shoes off and put them back on wet, because eventually Dad will notice I don't have any shoes.

After I change into the ridiculous gingerbread man costume, I grab a wad of paper towels and turn off the water. My hair protector survived, so I leave it on, just in case.

"Stay in here," I say to Gobbledy. "And hide if you hear anyone coming. I have to go back and wipe up the ketchup on the floor."

The ketchup trail leads down the hall to the big, metal doors. Leaning down, I put half the paper towels on the floor and push them forward with my hands. When I get to the production area, it's still empty. Excellent sign. I dump the ketchup-soaked paper towels in a trash can and pull more out. Big glops of ketchup sit in puddles around the base of the vat. I wipe and wipe until it's gone. Then I run back for Gobbledy and my backpack.

A set of wet, pink footprints, the size of Gobbledy's big feet, trail out of the bathroom and stop exactly eight steps away.

I shove the bathroom door open. "Gobbledy," I whisper loudly.

A wad of wet paper towels lies on the tile floor. Everything else is gone. No Gobbledy. No backpack. No Pet Rock carrier. I fling the door to each stall open.

Empty.

Empty.

Empty.

"Gobbledy," I say louder.

My only response is an echo.

I run back into the hall, look left, then right. I study the tracks. The whole factory is one big maze. I run down a hall and turn into another hall, then another. I stop and look back over my shoulder. How am I supposed to find him in this maze? I retrace my steps back to the main hall, and am about to check the production area, when I run smack into someone walking around the corner.

A security guard looks down at me. "Can I help you, Son?"

"I'm lost." I cringe.

"You can say that again. I've been looking everywhere for you for the last half-hour."

"Looking for me?" I ask.

I cross my fingers and pray there are no ketchup smears on my clothes.

"Follow me to the security desk."

"Am I in trouble?"

Someone clears their throat behind me. I turn.

Dougal stands in the middle of the hall, hair protector poofed out on his head. Squire Roberts stands next to him, holding a half-eaten sleeve of saltines.

"Oh," Squire says, "it seems we have a gypsy."

Huh?

"Gingerbread man," Dougal corrects.

Squire nods, "Oh, yeah. I can see it now. Gingerbread man. Right on."

"D-man," I blurt out, "I need some help."

Dougal whips the hair protector off his head and glares. "Where's your backpack with that new alien toy thingy you carry around?"

"We need to have a conference, pronto," I say.

Squire looks at us like we're nuts. "Okay. Good to see ya again. I have to go log the scores."

The security guard lays his hand on my shoulder, "We'll have this conference on the way to the security station."

Dougal leans close and whispers, "You're wearing a costume and don't have your trusty backpack. You have to admit, even for you, this is suspicious behavior."

"The Planetary Goons are here. I think they took Gobbledy *and* my backpack."

Dougal hisses under his breath, "What happened?"

"The Pet Rock carrier fell into a vat of ketchup. I left Gobbledy in the bathroom to clean my ketchup trail up, and when I went back, he was gone. His footprints ended a few feet outside the bathroom door."

"Are they still here?"

"I don't know. They're probably hiding." I swallow the panic in my voice. "They can't have Gobbledy. They'll put him in a cage and force him to live in their awful basement."

Up ahead, the security guard rounds the corner to the station.

Dougal straightens up tall and announces loudly, "I have to get something out of my dad's car before the babysitter gets here."

"The babysitter?" I ask.

"Dad called Fran to pick us up. Apparently, the people doing the big inspection showed up."

I think of Gobbledy and me swimming in the fresh ketchup, and cringe.

The guard furrows his brow, taking a seat in front of a row of monitors showing activity in different areas of the factory. My eyes trail from one grainy black-and-white screen to the next.

"Oh, my god," I say.

Dougal jerks his head around. "What?"

The guard stares at me, waiting, "Yes?"

"There's a bug on the console behind you," I say to the guard.

He turns around fast. As he does, I point to the monitor that shows the Planetary Goons walking across the parking lot. My backpack jerks from side to side as Gobbledy fights to get out.

Dougal gasps, "Sir, I really have to get something out of my dad's car."

The guard leans close to the console, checking every inch. "What kind of bug was it?"

"A big one," I yell, "that flies."

The guard jumps backwards, eyes still glued to the knobs and buttons.

Dougal jerks his head toward the back entrance and whispers, "Now."

In the parking lot, Dougal crouches down and runs alongside the cars, "Don't let them see you."

"I can run fast and snatch my backpack from his hand."

"They're too far," my little brother says, hunched over, crossing the aisle.

Desperate, I stand upright and yell, "Gobbledy! Run!"

The Planetary Goons turn to see who's yelling. All of a sudden, my backpack stops moving. The goon squeezes it tight. Gobbledy lets out a long, mournful yowl. The goons break into a run.

Gobbledy screams, muffled by the backpack.

"Chew your way out, Gobbledy," I scream. "Even if that is my favorite backpack, chew your way out."

The goons jump inside a blue car and start the engine. I am two rows away when the car lurches forward. Instead of backing up and exiting through the lot, they drive straight across a field that connects to the highway. The brake lights throw me into a complete panic.

They flash for a split second as the car speeds across the dried-up field next to the factory.

"Gobbledy!" I scream.

The car hesitates, rolls a few more feet, and one of the goons hits the gas. Dead grass and bits of dirt fly out from under the tires as it speeds away.

From me.

Forever.

I hitch up my gingerbread man pants and run.

As fast as I can. Eyes glued to the taillights.

I am determined to keep them in sight. The car bumps and jostles across uneven ground. Cold wind cuts straight through my gold and brown tunic.

Behind me, Dougal yells, "*What* are you *doing?*"

Without breaking stride, I yell, "We can't let them steal him. They'll lock him in a cage forever. They don't want him because they love him. They just think he'll make them famous."

I stumble across dry, clumpy ground. Dust catches in my throat. I heave forward, coughing. Taillights travel farther and farther away. I wave the dust away, trying to see. My foot slams into a rock, and I go hurtling through the air. I land with a loud thump on my chest and can't catch my breath. I wheeze and moan, reaching for the fading taillights. The world goes gray around the edges and I cough one last, wretched time. With only a few seconds left I try to focus on the license plate. MCL 418. *Wham.* My face hits the ground, and my dusty world goes black.

The sun is setting on the horizon, dark and low.

Fi pops her gum, looking down at me. "Someone call for a ride?"

Dougal is crouched down beside her, checking my vitals. "Do you need medical attention?"

I sit up and cough. "For what?"

"You knocked yourself out," Fi says, holding her palm up for a high five.

A dark, woozy sensation greets me as I try to stand. "Where's my backpack?"

Dougal fills his cheeks with air, then exhales. "The Planetary Goons got it."

I snatch the hair protector off my head.

"Come on," Fi says, "Your dad called my sister and asked if she'd babysit. She's waiting in the parking lot. Let's get back to my house and see if we can outsmart these jerks."

Dougal pulls me to my feet. "By the looks of them, it can't be that hard."

Twenty-Eight

Fi flops down into a creaky desk chair on wheels and fires up a computer. She types the license plate number into a box and presses enter. "Hmm. . . ." she says, hunkered over the keyboard. "Your MCL 418 license plate is to a rental car."

"Can we find out the name of the person who rented it?" Dougal asks.

She shakes her head. "Not without hacking into the rental car system, and Daddy freaks out when me and Fran do that." Fi cocks her head and eyes me strangely. "What are you supposed to be?"

Before I have a chance to answer, Dougal says, "Gingerbread man. Can't you see the resemblance?"

Fi crinkles her nose. "You're in the Winter Extravaganza? Why didn't you tell me? That's terrible. I'd get my dad to write me a note."

I look down at my costume. "I didn't tell you because it happened so fast. I can't get out of it. I have to be on stage tonight." Frantically, I dust pieces of dry grass onto the basement floor.

Fi raises an eyebrow. "That's a bit of a time constraint." Pushing back from the desk, she frowns, "We need some way to track their movements."

"My warp speed device," I blurt out.

Rolling his eyes, Dougal says, "It doesn't really work."

"It kinda does. I made it from Dad's old work phone."

Fi claps her hands together. "I remember that thing. If it's a phone, then it has a GPS inside. Is it charged?"

"As far as I know. Dad had an extended life battery for it, so one charge lasts forever. It's in the front zipper compartment of my backpack."

Fi rubs her hands together. "Okay, what was the telephone number associated with that device? I'll see what kind of magic I can work. In the meantime, make yourselves at home. And don't you ever tell Daddy I let you come down here."

Daddy has all kinds of stuff. Real night-vision goggles, flak jackets, pens with cameras inside.

Fi does a victory spin in her chair. "Got it."

Dougal drops a digital recorder shaped like a salt-shaker back into its box, and we both run over. Fi points at the computer screen. "See that flashing green dot?"

We nod in unison.

"That's your backpack."

D-man and I steal a glance. "That's all the way across town."

"Hold on. Let me synch up one of Daddy's old laptops, and we'll take it with us."

"What does it mean if it's just flashing, and not moving?"

"It means those scumbags who stole your backpack stopped to catch their breath." Fi closes her laptop, tucks it under her arm, and runs for the stairs, "Hold on. Let me ask my sister if she'll drive."

The four of us skid to a stop at Fran's Festiva. Fran jerks the driver's door open. Dry leaves skitter across the sidewalk. Streetlights click on up and down the block. I shiver. Time is ticking.

The dark of winter sets in as the Festiva zooms down the boulevard with all of us crammed inside.

Fi glances back over her shoulder. "See how I have a bunch of windows open on the laptop?"

Dougal and I look over her shoulder.

"One of those programs cross-references the GPS with an address for the green dot. I'm going to see if I can get a location."

The Festiva whizzes past bare trees and plastic snowflakes mounted on telephone poles.

If we don't get to Gobbledy fast, the Planetary Goons will take away his milk bottle and his rock, and there will be no hope of ever finding him again.

"Got it," Fi announces.

"Give me the address," Fran instructs.

"It's umm . . . It's a route number."

"A what?"

"You know, one of those addresses that's way out in the country."

Fran glances at her sister. "Are you sure?"

Fi's face glows in the laptop screen. "Totally sure."

Fran slams her foot down on the gas. "All right then. Give me a lock down on our target."

"Lock down in progress," Fi says as she types furiously.

Twenty-Nine

The small, two-lane road narrows to a single-lane dirt road. Fran slows the Festiva, bumping along. Skeletal brown corn stalks stretch out on either side.

Fran glances at her sister. "Give me an update, Fi. Are we still on target?"

I'm frozen in my seat, waiting.

Fi's eyes search the screen. "According to the signal, yes."

I turn, craning my neck to look back down the road. A dark sky casts no shadows. I shiver.

Fi lays her hand on the dash. My eyes sweep across the path, illuminated by the headlights. "I seriously hope this isn't a trap. This makes my creepy meter flash like crazy."

Dust rises in the cold air. A single raindrop plops on the windshield.

Craning his neck, Dougal looks up. "Just what we need."

Fran shrugs. "I'll take rain. It's supposed to snow."

"We're coming up to the signal kinda fast," Fi says.

I squeeze my hands together and will Gobbledy back

to me. We are almost there. *Hold on, little alien dude.*
Help is on the way.

The Festiva putters along.

"I think you need to stop," Fi says. "Stop *now!*"

Fran's foot slams on the brakes. The Festiva lurches
to a halt, throwing us all forward.

Fi's eyes focus on something crumpled in the middle
of the road. Squinting to get a better look, she whispers,
"What is going on?"

I push my way out of the back seat and run to the
middle of the dirt road. There, on the ground, sits the
loneliest sight in the world.

My dusty, rumpled, ketchup-stained backpack.

All alone.

Abandoned by thieves.

I snatch it up fast and pull the zipper open. Headlights illuminate the inside. A few folded pieces of
homework. One used pink eraser. One monster decal,
because you never know when you'll need one of those
on the spot. One empty Cheesy Twister bag. One lone
milk bottle.

And nothing else.

I unzip the front compartment and feel around. A
second later, I pull out my warp speed device. For a single instant I consider the implications. Then, I press the
activate button, hoping to launch myself far enough into
the future to find Gobbledy.

Thunder rumbles in the dark sky. I press the button
again. When nothing happens, I drop the device on the

ground and turn my backpack upside down. The contents tumble onto the dirt. Fi and Dougal step out of the car, leaving the door open. I look down at my ketchup-stained tennis shoes and want to cry.

Dougal walks up behind me, asking quietly, "Anything?"

I shake my head, turning in a complete circle because I can't believe this is true. My eyes scan the fields. "*Gobbledy!*" I scream as loud as I can.

Fran cocks her head out of the driver's window. "What are you doing? Isn't this your backpack?"

Dougal clears his throat. "He had this insect thingy he found in the forest."

"Oh," Fran considers this information. "He had a bug in there?"

He isn't just a bug. Or even a thingy. He's my friend, and the idea that I am just going to leave him behind is wrong. I take off down the rows of dried stalks, wailing, "Gobbledy!" The corn leaves slap me hard, but I run, looking for footprints.

"Dexter, wait!" Fi yells behind me. "We have to stay together."

Drops of rain fall from the sky. I search the ground for clues. Broken leaves, disturbed dirt, anything that signals Gobbledy may have been here first. He couldn't have gone far, clutching his Pet Rock carrier.

Behind me, Dougal shouts, "Gobbledy. Come on, little dude. We've got snacks."

"You named the insect?" Fran yells.

"You know Dexter. He names everything."

"Okay, fair enough," she says. "Gobbledy. Come out. Come out. Wherever you are."

For a split second the moon bursts out from behind a thick covering of clouds. Cold rain patters down in a steady stream. Water washes away tracks. I have to hurry. In the distance, I see the figure of a man. I can tackle him and bring him to the ground. Clods of dirt crumble under my feet.

"Gobbledy!" I yell.

"Gobbledy!" Dougal yells.

"Gobbledy!" Fi yells.

No one answers. The man doesn't turn. Maybe he can't hear us because of the rain. A loud clap of lightning rips across the sky. Rain soaks my hair and tunic. I trip on uneven ground and fall face first into the dirt.

"You stole him," I scream. Tears burn hot in my eyes.

I push myself up and run toward the man, crossing row after row. Rain falls harder, turning cold. The moon disappears behind thick clouds. I run with a single, solid hope: that Gobbledy is one row over, chirping and chattering and waiting to go home. I break through the final row and stumble, muddy and wet, right into the man. I look up. For a split second the scarecrow's painted eyes reflect a bolt of lightning ripping the sky in half.

Windshield wipers slap the rain. I ride with my head squeezed out Fi's window, frantically calling for Gobbledy.

Fi clears her throat. "Dexter?"

When I don't answer, Dougal says, "It's six thirty-three."

"Maybe he can't hear me because of the rain," I yell back over my shoulder.

Fi grabs my arm. "He's not out here."

I spin around quick, "You don't know that."

"Yes. I do. He sticks to you like glue. If he was out here, we would have found him."

Fran slows to a stop and puts the car in park. "Listen. I promise I will bring you back out here after the play."

The thought is unbearable. "That means he'll be out in the cold rain for hours."

"Look," Fi says, "I want to find him just as much as you do, but I don't see the point of searching for him if he isn't here. We have to find him. This will give me more time to search and see what I come up with."

Furrowing her brow tight, Fran sighs and says, "It's going to be a bad scene if your dad is sitting in that auditorium, wondering why you're not on stage. He called me and asked me to pick you two up and deliver you safely to the play. He's going to be really mad if I don't keep my word."

Dougal, the little voice of reason, nods. "Not showing up guarantees Code Red."

I hold my breath. I can't leave him out in the cold, dark rain.

Fran points to the clock on her dash. "Show time is in seventeen minutes, and the GPS says it takes twenty-five minutes to get to the front door of the auditorium."

Thirty

Two Gingerbread Men are on stage under a bright yellow beam, cast down from the ceiling. The rest of the stage is black. I shove my legs into a pair of pants I find on a rack and feel around in the dark for a shirt. All I know is, I cannot take the stage wearing a dirty, ripped costume. My dad is somewhere out in the audience, ready to slide that magnet on my behavior chart right to Code Red.

Classmates in blue-and-white snowflake costumes glance nervously around the stage, but no one says, "The Gingerbread Men bring gifts of laughter and cheer."

One of the Gingerbread Men turns and stares at me, jerking his thumb toward the stage. My ketchup-stained tennis shoe is stuck in my pant leg. I hop around, trying to break free.

A cough echoes through the auditorium. Then another. A low murmur kicks up. From this angle, I can see Fi and Fran and Dougal sneak quietly into the dark auditorium. The Snow King spots me and waves frantically.

The shoe will not come off. I grab a robe off a hanger,

whip it over my shoulders and half-limp, half-run onto the stage in a thundering blur. A moment of breathless silence quivers in the audience. I look down. The golden tassels on my robe glint in the stage light.

The Snow King wraps his arms around the snow-man and says, "Two Gingerbread Men and a pirate have come to bring us winter cheer."

A loud, collective gasp explodes in the auditorium.

"He has come for our gold," the first Gingerbread Man yells, "and our good booty."

Wild applause erupts. A cacophony of jeers and laughter kicks up.

"You have sailed the seven seas to be here on this magical night," the Snow Queen yells over the noise.

One Gingerbread Man offers, "And taken no prison-ers."

I pull a sword attached to my robe out, holding it high. "Aye, matey. Winter break is finally here."

Miss Watson steps up to the curtain, wags an angry fist, and stomps out onto the stage, presumably to re-move me. I squeeze my eyes shut and take a step back, not looking forward to whatever follows.

Suddenly, loud whoops erupt from the audience.

I crack an eye open.

Miss Watson stops in the middle of the stage and turns to face the audience. People cheer and clap. Out of the corner of her eye, Miss Watson glares at me a split second, then turns to the audience and dips into a sweeping bow.

The room gives way to a thunder of laughter.

"I hope someone videotaped that spectacle." The Snow King sputters, half laughing, half talking.

A breath catches in my throat.

Videotape? I'd been in such a rush to get on stage I didn't think about that. Oh, God. There must be dozens. It's the Winter Embarrassment. Every parent in the world came to record the talents of their adorable children.

The Snow Queen whispers, "I hope we can get copies."

With the attention finally off me, I try to wrestle my shoe out of the pant leg. Dad is in the middle of the third row, eyes wide. The audience rises into a standing ovation. Miss Watson bows again. I pray a hole will open up in the stage and swallow me forever. Like Gobbledy. Who is going to spend the rest of his life in a cage. In a dark basement. Held captive by two creepy amateur alien hunters, who are going to force him to do dumb tricks for clicks on YouTube.

Without his milk bottle.

Snarly turns on me the second the faded, red curtain hits the stage. With that crooked tooth glinting in the light, she points her finger and hisses, "You little troublemaker. You veered from the script."

I turn to run, but The Snow King yells, "That was awesome."

The curtain jerks and starts curling up again. Snarly swings back around to face the audience. A great roar rises up from the rows of seats, filled with friends and family. The walls shake.

In the dim light, I see Fi with her finger jammed in one ear, and her phone pressed to the other. Dougal stares at me like I'm a freak. Dad stares at me like I'm from outer space, and claps slowly.

The Gingerbread Men, Candy Cane Chorus, and Snow King and Queen all swoop forward into a deep bow. Flashes on phones light up the audience. Snarly turns to me, a fake smile stretched ear to ear, and says, "Take a bow, Duckworth. Before I end you."

With my shoe still stuck in my pant leg, I limp forward awkwardly and bend over. People cheer and yell and whistle and whoop so loud I can't hear my heart thundering in my ears anymore. All of those smiling, laughing faces temporarily melt my distress. When the curtain begins to lower, Snarly Watson steps forward, determined to make the glory last. I slide quietly sideways until the curtain hits the stage.

As the backdoor slams shut behind me, I hear one of the volunteers say, "I wish my kids were that interesting. All they ever do is sit on the couch and play video games. . . ."

Wham.

Cold air slaps my hot cheeks. I stumble across the athletic field with one shoe stuck in my pant leg. While I was inside embarrassing myself, it started to snow, because I currently don't have enough obstacles in my life. A cold drizzle seeps through my costume and makes me shiver. I look left, then right, trying to remember where we parked. Holding onto one of the bleachers, I wrestle my ketchup-stained shoe off, but lose my balance and step on the wet ground. Cold grass soaks my toes.

I hop around, thrusting my hand down my pants leg, pulling off my slimy tennis shoe. I look up in time to see Fi crossing the parking lot, staring down at her phone. Parents and kids begin filing out of the auditorium in waves.

"Hurry up," I yell, "before my dad finds me and grounds me forever."

Fran looks at me, "Where to?"

"Back to the cornfield. Maybe Gobbledy got away and is hiding out there."

Fran flips her seat forward so I can climb into the back.

Fi holds up her hand. "Hold on. I might have another destination."

Dougal catches up to us as I climb into the backseat. "Sorry. I had to dodge Dad."

Fi jumps into the front seat and fires up her laptop.

After a few seconds of clicking, Fi holds the screen up so everyone can see it.

Fran squints, "What am I looking at?"

"Oh, my god," Dougal says, recognizing the place.

Fi looks at Fran. "I set up cameras in the forest to create a video of what animals do in their natural habitat, for a school project. The cameras have sensors, and every time the sensor is tripped, I get a notification."

"So?"

"So, the goons who stole my backpack are in the forest," I say breathlessly.

Fi points at the screen. "On camera."

Fran fires up the Festiva. "You need to screenshot that and send it to Daddy. In the meantime, give me some coordinates."

"The forest near the playground," Fi says.

On screen, Planetary Goons search under a blanket of fallen leaves for rocks. My eyes scan the dark, but I don't see a little green night-vision Gobbledy.

I strap my seatbelt on as Fran gives it gas, throwing us back in our seats.

Glancing up into the rearview mirror, she asks, "What exactly were you supposed to be in that play back there?"

Dougal rolls his eyes. "Grounded."

Fi points at the screen. "Hurry up. They're moving out of range."

Thirty-One

The parking lot next to the playground is empty except for one car. *The goon car.* The one I saw parked outside our house.

My heart beats really fast. "They have Gobbledy, and we're going to have to take them."

"With what?" Dougal chokes.

"Listen, we can't take them," Fran says.

"There's four of us, and two of them," I point out.

"Five, if you count Gobbledy," Fi says, overly hopeful.

"Trust me, I am the biggest one in our group, and I doubt I can take them. We'll have to outsmart them."

"How?" Dougal wants to know.

"I don't know exactly."

"Not to point out the obvious, but we don't have a lot of time," I add.

"I know. I know," Fran says, feeling the pinch.

The snow is accumulating. Two sets of fresh tracks lead from the rental car, across the bridge, and into the woods, but they are disappearing fast. It's so quiet I can hear everyone breathing. The windows fog up.

Suddenly Fi says, "The car."

No one moves.

Finally, I ask, "What about the car?"

"Their car. We should try and search their car. See if Gobbledy is locked inside."

"Best idea ever." I push at the back of Fran's seat. "Let me out."

Fran throws her door open and jumps out. I follow, stepping into snow up to my ankles. It's not enough that I am wearing a flimsy pirate costume, or that my tennis shoes are wet with ketchup. Now, I have to be ankle-deep in snow.

"Okay, guys," Fran says, "what, exactly, are we looking for?"

Fi, Dougal, and I stare at each other in the streetlight. Snowflakes stick to Fi's eyelashes.

She looks at her sister and says, "It's this weird little animal that looks like a cross between a prairie dog, a chinchilla, and a cartoon."

Fran stops to consider the description. "I thought you said it was an insect."

"Or a rock," Dougal adds. "Sometimes it looks like a rock.'

"A rock?" Fran asks.

"Go with it," Fi instructs.

"We don't have much time," I say, running around the car, looking in all the windows. No Gobbledy.

"Let's see if we can get the trunk open," Fi says.

I know Gobbledy isn't in the trunk. If he were, he'd be yelling to me right now. I take off in the direction of the bridge. "I'm going to find him."

"Wait," Fran yells. "The snow is really coming down. I don't know how much longer it will be safe to drive. We have to stay together."

The snow isn't as thick in the forest because of the trees, but it's freezing. I follow the prints to the clearing where Fi set up cameras. The area is empty. I want to yell out Gobbledy's name, but I don't want to tip off the goons. My fingers and toes are so cold they ache. My teeth chatter. This is why Mom always told me to wear my coat. I look back toward the parking lot and realize the snow is giving me away. My footprints leave a path. I fumble under the leaves, grasping for stones, but they crumble to dust in my hands.

Someone asks behind me, "Where's the animal from outer space?"

"What?" I spin around. The two goons stand on the path, holding nets and rope.

"I—I don't know," I stammer, feeling cold and trapped.

"You know where it is," the other one says.

Even in the dark, I can see they aren't professionals. They're just two overweight guys with big heads and scraggily ponytails. They are five feet away and inching forward. I back up.

"Where is the spaceship debris?"

"What?"

"If this is a real alien, then where is the crash debris? We know you found it."

I shrug. "How am I supposed to know? We didn't

look for any debris. There were just these mushroom things, and we were trying to figure out what they were, before they disintegrated."

The biggest goon tilts his head. "Mushroom things?"

It suddenly occurs to me that a) I have said too much, and b) If they are asking me questions then one thing is certain: they know absolutely nothing.

"Where's my friend?" I yell.

The smaller goon has a nose like a beak. "Come with us," he says. "We'll show you where he is."

The big goon walks toward me.

I back up, stumbling over piles of leaves.

"You should come with us."

Neither one is holding a bag or pack or anything. It suddenly occurs to me that they have no clue where Gobbledy is, either. He must have gotten loose. I spin around and take off running.

They're not professionals.

They're a viral video plague.

Trying to steal the spotlight, and my best friend.

"Wait a minute," one goon yells.

The other one yells, "Don't let him get away."

I hear their footsteps behind me in the quiet forest. I know this forest like I know my own house. I've spent years out here. I might not be able to outrun them, but I can find somewhere to hide. I run over knobby tree roots and fallen logs. I run as fast as I can, listening for the sound of the river. As long as I can find the river, I can find my way back. I run faster, tree after tree whizzing past me. I run until I can't hear them chasing me anymore. I run, and I am just about to sneak a glance back over my shoulder, when my wet sneaker hits a slippery tree root and launches me into the air.

I reach out to grab a limb, but there is nothing. My other foot slides out from under me. I hit the ground and *wham*! Snow seeps through my costume for a split second before my head hits a log, and I am out.

Thirty-Two

Snowflakes drift down through the tree branches like a lullaby. I watch them a few seconds before I realize I am on the ground covered in snow. Clouds pass in front of the moon. I hear a single, unmistakable grunt. Gobbledy slaps me on the cheek. I sit up, freezing, and have no idea how long I've been out.

"Gobbledy!" I yell.

The lone figure looks at me, face hidden in shadows. His fur is caked with mud, soaking wet, and his teeth chatter ferociously. One of his ears is horribly bent.

"Oh, my god," I whisper, trying to stand. "What happened to you?"

The cold makes his whole body tremble. He holds his arms out to the sides, palms open. I can barely see him in the dark. Slowly and gently, he moves his arms, so they rest in front of his chest. Opening and closing his hands he looks up at me, big tears forming in his eyes. It takes me a second, but suddenly I realize what's going on.

Gobbledy bursts into tears.

Snowflakes flutter down to the ground.

I lift Gobbledy off the ground. Sobbing uncontrollably, he lets his wet forehead smack against my chest.

I wrap my arms around him to keep him warm as he
sucks in a long breath and yowls.

By the time I reach the bridge, I'm so cold I can't stop
shaking. Gobbledy lies limp in my arms. I have never
been so relieved to see Fran's car.

"They waited on us," I blurt out.

Gobbledy looks up but doesn't make a noise.

The goon car is gone. Snow covers the parking lot. I
squint to see if everyone is piled into Fran's Festiva.
When I realize it's empty, I look around desperately.

"Fi!" I yell. "Dougal!"

I worry that the goons did something before they
left. Something not very nice at all. I am so cold, my
head pounds.

"Fi!" I yell. "Fi!"

I am just about to give up when I hear a muffled
voice say, "*Help me!*"

"What?"

"Help me!"

The second cry for help is followed by pounding on
a door. I look around. A simple turn of the head makes
my cold bones feel like they're breaking.

Then I hear Dougal's voice, small and faint, but unmistakable. "Dexter? Is that you? Help us!"

Without lifting his head, Gobbledy points to the parks and recreational building, where the bathrooms and vending machines are located.

"I'm coming," I yell. "Where are you?"

"In the bathroom," Fi and Fran yell. "We're locked in the bathroom."

I am thinking I will have to climb through a window, or pick a lock, when I get to the door and realize it locks from the outside. Gobbledy reaches down and turns the lock, because I am too frozen to move.

Fran bursts out of the dark bathroom. "Oh, my god."

Dougal eyes my wet costume. "Your lips are blue."

"I need a blanket," I say.

Fi grabs Gobbledy and pulls off her coat, handing it over to me. "When we saw the goons coming back to the car, we ran and hid in here. They must have seen our footprints, because they locked us in the bathroom. What took you so long?"

I rub the back of my head. "I fell down."

Fran pulls her scarf and hat off and hands them over to me. "We've been locked in here for hours."

Gobbledy looks up at Fi. "You're a mess," she says. "What happened to you?"

He holds out his empty hands.

No one says a word.

No one understands.

He bursts into tears.

"They stole his rock," I say.

🎁

The backseat of the Festiva is warm, with Gobbledy stuffed down in my backpack. I hug him close. A cold wind kicks up. Snowflakes melt on the windshield like tears.

"Okay, listen," Dougal says, rubbing his hands together to keep warm. "We can fix this situation."

Gobbledy squeezes his milk bottle so tight it crinkles.

Dougal puts his hands in front of the heaters to warm up. "If Dad is home, we're going to have a hard time explaining why your backpack cries uncontrollably."

I glare at him. "He saved me. I could have frozen to death out there."

"That's not my point. My point is that this missing rock business has created a bit of a situation."

"Stop being so logical."

Moonlight splashes across the sidewalk for a brief second as clouds open up.

"We have to figure out what to do," Dougal insists. "We can't just walk into our house and wing it. It's too risky. What if those guys are waiting for us?"

Gobbledy blubbers inside my pack, his bottle crinkling with each sob. My legs ache, my stomach grumbles. The dark streets are so quiet I can hear the soft wet patter of snowflakes hitting the pavement. My breath fogs beneath my nostrils. I am freezing and tired and want to get home.

"Okay, so what do we do?"

"You're the older, wiser brother. You tell me."

I consider this bit of sarcasm a brief moment.

Dougal huffs. "Ask Gobbledy if there's something we can do."

I stare at my little brother. For as smart and funny as he can be, he's totally clueless at times. I clear my throat. "I am just happy he's alive. I'll stay grounded forever if I have to."

Dougal's face pinches in concern.

The streets are empty. It's weird, riding in a car, driving twenty miles per hour in a snowstorm, dressed as a pirate, squeezing my sobbing backpack.

Thirty-Three

The sight at the top of the stairs does not instill hope.

"What's wrong?" I ask Dougal.

He stands in our doorway, white-faced, mouth open.

Gobbledy pops his head out of my backpack. His scraggly, wet ears twitch.

"Hold on," I whisper. Then to Dougal, I urge, "What is going on?"

Unable to speak, D-man simply points to our bedroom and steps aside to let me pass. I walk into our bedroom, looking around for the source of Dougal's distress.

The top of our dresser is empty.

Gobbledy grabs the zipper on my pack, trying to pull himself out.

I spin around.

Dougal stands dazed in the doorway. "They stole our collection cups," he stammers.

"But—" My eyes search the room.

My little brother turns to me, "The goons came back here, and stole our samples."

I set my backpack on the dresser and drop to the

floor. An old baseball bat and a few socks mingle with dust bunnies under my bed, but no collection cups.

When I lift my head, Dougal points at Gobbledy standing on the dresser, "I lined them up right there."

I look under Dougal's bed anyway. It's very tidy. No toys or clothes or dust. I sit down, take off my wet pirate costume, and kick off my wet tennis shoes. Dark, oddly shaped blotches of ketchup stain the sides. I pull on my pajamas and my coat and hat and mittens. Dougal stares at me.

I shrug, teeth chattering. "I don't have any clean clothes."

A sniffling starts. I jerk my head around. Big tears form in Gobbledy's eyes as he holds out his empty hands.

"It's okay," I jump to my feet.

Dougal shakes his head. "It's not okay. They stole our hard work."

I snatch Gobbledy up fast and run for the attic door. He quivers in my arms, letting out a tiny gasp before diving headlong into the loudest wail I've ever heard.

In the attic, I tune an old radio into a station to drown out the sobs of a lonely alien without its rock. Gobbledy frees himself from my grip and limps over to the sofa, dragging his misshapen milk bottle.

Dougal takes the stairs two at a time.

The radio crackles with static. The Tim & Bob Evening Show is on.

"And so, Tim, this kid . . ." Bob pauses because he's laughing so hard. "And so, these two kids walk out onto the stage, dressed up in their gingerbread men get-ups. But the audience just sits there, because there's supposed to be three gingerbread men, right?"

"It's that way every year," Tim snickers.

"But there's not. So, I'm sitting there waiting to see if one of the gingerbread men has called in sick, or maybe there have been cutbacks at the old Cookie Factory. God knows the layoffs have been terrible lately."

Tim and Bob hoot.

"So, I'm sitting in my seat on the third row," Bob continues. "And this kid comes running out onto the stage, dressed as a pirate."

Tim's tone drops to incredulous. "No."

"Really. It was the funniest thing I've ever seen." Bob blurts out, "Then, one of the kids yells, 'Give me your good booty.' I swear."

"Apparently, the third gingerbread man was captured by pirates." Tim howls.

I jerk the knob across the dial, stopping on a new station, where a woman's voice says, "And in other local news, there was mayhem to be had during a holiday production, but luckily the baby snowman was unharmed. Now, Kim, back to you for the weather. I hear there's a blizzard headed our way."

I snap the radio off.

News coverage is high profile. Dad should be at work, where thankfully there are no radios. Except in the break room, but Dad never takes breaks. Dougal rounds the corner at the top of the stairs, dragging his feet. Gobbledy flops back against the sofa. It's fairly obvious I'm going to have to be the glue that holds Kissmas together.

"Knock, knock," Dad calls up the stairs.

Dougal jerks his eyes to Gobbledy, still crying on the sofa. "Yes?"

"Can I come up?"

I toss a blanket over Gobbledy and pray he doesn't howl.

Dad stops in the doorway, stooped over so he doesn't bang his head on the low ceiling.

I watch the blanket. So far, so good. The blanket is not currently crying.

"I came up here to see if you're hungry," he says.

I perk up at the mention of food, but I am suspicious that no one is yelling at me.

Dad stares at Mom's amazing village. Little park benches, miniature potted plants, and beautiful handmade trees. His finger trails down a cobbled street to The Tavern, his eyes travel the distance of the town, past the drugstore and the movie theater, to the edge of the forest. A quaint dirt path curves its way through the miniature trees. Looking closer, he spots tiny owls in tree branches, raccoons on the path, squirrels standing next to wooden buckets full of tiny nuts. A little miniature hand-carved Gobbledy I've never seen before. He must have done that while I was out.

Ding dong.

The blanket shudders. Dad looks at me and Dougal.

Ding dong.

"Hold on. I'll be right back," Dad says. "I want to talk to you."

The blanket quivers and sobs.

Dad stops. "What was that?"

Dougal looks straight up at him and says, "Dexter. It's a new ventriloquist routine he's working on."

"Huh." He turns his attention to me. "You're such a weird kid, but you show such initiative."

I shrug. That's me. Mr. Special. Mr. Initiative.

As soon as he leaves the attic, I thrust a granola bar under the blanket. Gobbledy drops it listlessly onto the floor.

Dougal sighs. "Go try to keep Dad downstairs. This is a time-bomb ticking."

"We can work this out, D-man."

"Those were my favorite collection cups."

"I'll buy more with my allowance."

Dougal jerks his head around and glares at me. "I want mine back." He pushes himself upright and grabs Dad's old laptop. "In fact, I am sending those jerks an email and demanding my cups back. This is no way to conduct business. They are in no way acting professional. I'm going to call their parents and get them kicked out of their basement."

"Okay. I am going to see what's going on downstairs."

Gobbledy sniffles, then falls on his side, howling.

Thirty-Four

Dad unlatches the door and throws it open.

I hide at the top of the stairs, and gasp in horror.

On the front steps, Snarly Watson stands, angry and wobbly, supported on either side by crutches.

"Good evening," she growls.

When Dad fails to choke out a reply, Miss Watson clears her throat, "Is your family home?"

Dad shakes his head slowly, like he isn't sure.

"Very well," Miss Watson frowns. "I'll make do with you."

Dad steps aside for fear of being mowed down by an angry, injured middle school principal.

Snarly clacks down the hall, stopping at the doorway to the living room. "Hurry up," she instructs, then clanks out of sight.

After closing the front door, Dad doesn't move. I am certain he should run.

Snarly Watson huffs eight times.

Finally, Dad smooths his ketchup-stained jacket, takes a deep breath, and walks into the living room. "Hi," he says, too quick to be sincere.

Snarly clears her throat and starts, "I should get right down to the reason for my visit. I want to know what kind of people let a little monster like that bring a pirate costume to ruin my Winter Extravaganza."

"Well . . ." Dad begins.

I creep down the top four stairs so I can hear better. Here it comes. *Code Red.*

Snarly drums her fingernails against her crutch.

"The truth is that I didn't know he was going to be a pirate. I didn't even know about the extravaganza thing until the last minute. Things have been a little difficult lately. . . ."

I slide quietly down the stairs to peek around the corner, into the living room.

"I mean, I guess I should have known because—"

"Because he's so devious?"

"No," Dad blurts. "Because your Winter Extravaganza is even more boring now than when I was in school."

Oh. My. God. Go. Dad.

Snarly doesn't flinch. "Well, I certainly didn't want him in my production. Now look where it's gotten me." She points a bony finger at her injured leg.

I grimace.

"I didn't see anything happen while he was on stage that would have caused you to hurt your leg," Dad says.

Ninth and tenth huff.

"That's because I slipped on a wet gingerbread costume backstage. It was flung across the floor in the dark. I was annoyed and distracted, which would not have been the case if my artfully crafted choir and Snow Queen routine had not been ruined. Even so, that was your son's costume. The one he'd been instructed to guard with his life."

"I am sure he has a reason. Maybe it got wet when he was running into the auditorium."

Miss Watson's face twists into a frown. "He always has a reason, and the reason is because he's bad."

Here it comes. Code Red on the horizon.

"Complicated and headstrong, but he's not bad. He's just—"

Snarly leans forward, interrupting, "Bad."

Dad stands abruptly. "You know, Carlotta Watson, I have a lot to do tonight. My son lost his mother six months ago, and I am terribly sorry you've been inconvenienced by our family falling apart during this holiday season. Thank you for stopping by."

Not.

Snarly doesn't budge. She remains on the sofa, staring up at Dad with her piercing, hard eyes. "I don't think you'll thank me when you hear what I have to say."

Dad's voice quivers, "Go ahead."

The principal's face twists into a grin. Her crooked tooth gleams in the light of the pink Kissmas tree. "I have considered expelling Dexter Duckworth."

The word *expel* explodes in my head.

Code Red. Code Red. Red Alert. Code Red.

"What? You can't. . . ." Dad stammers.

"You're right. It seems I can't. The school's code of conduct informs me that my beloved extravaganza is considered extracurricular, which means Dexter Duckworth didn't actually disobey school policy. He disobeyed me. So the school cannot take drastic action against him. The good news is that your wretched little boy will have to be absolutely perfect for the rest of the year. If he forgets to cross a T, I will penalize him. If he disturbs class in any way, I will write him up. If he breathes too loud, he will spend his entire time in the hall with his nose up against the wall. I will do everything in my power to make sure that no fun is had at my expense. Ever. Again."

"I'm sure you will," Dad motions toward the front door. "It's nice to see you haven't changed a bit. Now, if you'll excuse me, I have to get back to what I was doing."

Snarly frowns but hoists herself up anyway.

I bolt ninja-fast up the stairs.

Snarly crutches down the hall.

Without hesitation, Dad flings the front door open, pointing to the front yard. "I'm sure you have better things to do."

Snarly Watson clacks past onto the front porch and stops. Without turning around, she wonders aloud, "I can't imagine how a little boy learned to be so bad. It must have been—"

The rest of the sentence is cut short by the door

slamming shut. Dad dusts his hands off and says out loud, "You are the meanest principal I've ever met."

"I heard that," Snarly yells from the other side of the door.

Chills run down my spine. Crutches clack down the front steps. Dad shudders and locks the door.

I run for the attic.

Dougal is sitting on the floor, staring up at Gobbledy on the sofa.

As soon as I bound around the corner, Dougal turns. "Dexter, we've got a problem."

My eyes roll back in my head. "I'm in crisis control mode right now. Snarly Watson just tried to expel me. I am literally *seconds* away from Code Red."

Ping. Ping.

Dougal clears his throat. "It won't compare to this."

Ping. Ping.

Gobbledy cocks his head to the side and stares at the window.

Ping. Ping. Ping.

I walk over and open the window. Cold air blows in, sending shivers right down to my toes.

Below, in the backyard, Fi whispers and waves up to me, "We've got a new development."

Thirty-Five

Fi stands on the back porch wearing the pink sequined coat that matches her purple cowboy boots. A blanket of fresh, white snow covers the backyard. The cold burst of air makes my head ache. "Please tell me they didn't steal the piece of craft we hid in your basement."

"It's still there. I checked."

"Are you okay?"

Shifting a canvas shopping bag on her shoulder, Fi thrusts out her pinky finger and whispers, "We're gonna have to pinky swear on this one."

Hesitantly, I hook my pinky in hers, wondering what I'm getting into.

She glances at the kitchen window behind me, then swings the bag off her shoulder. Inside, the rock glows, faint but golden.

The sight takes my breath away. Maybe I'm cold. Maybe I'm exhausted. Maybe I am totally nuts, but I have never been so happy to see a rock in all my life.

I reach down into the bag, moving Dougal's collection cups to the side, and touch it gently. "How did you get this stuff back?"

Fi lowers her voice even more. "We're going to file this as highly classified, Dex-Man. I called Daddy, and he traced the car to the airport. The Planetary Goons were returning their rental car. Daddy intercepted. In order to press charges, he'd have to notify your dad, which I was pretty sure you didn't want to do in this lifetime, so he snagged the contraband and dropped it off."

"But how did he know?"

Fi roots around in the canvas bag, retrieving a collection cup. Turning it over, I see: Property of Dougal Duckworth printed on the bottom, in black permanent marker.

My uptight little brother who doesn't want people to touch his stuff saved Gobbledy's rock.

Handing over the canvas bag, Fi whispers, "This is going to be our secret. Got it?"

I nod and toss the strap over my shoulder.

Fi steps back and says, "You'd better get inside. Your dad is staring at us through the window."

My stomach drops to my knees, and I feel light-headed. Stalling, I say, "I'm pretty sure I go straight to Code Red the second I walk inside."

Fi's face pinches into a frown. "What? It's winter break."

"Yeah, well, I've been avoiding this moment all week."

Fi sighs loudly, but then rushes forward, kissing my cheek. Her face is warm against mine as she whispers, "Merry Kissmas."

Unsure as to what to say, I smile awkwardly and say, "You, too."

Fi gives me a wave before running down the back steps, where her boots leave footprints in the snow.

Almost Kissmas snow.

Unable to procrastinate any longer, I turn around and pull the back door open to meet Angry Dad.

The warm kitchen is nice.

Dad just stares at me.

I squeeze my eyes shut, preparing for Code Red.

He clears his throat, and I cringe.

"Well," he starts.

Good-bye, freedom.

Hello, Code Red.

"It looks like Kissmas hasn't been laid off or met with corporate cutbacks. That in itself is a miracle."

I crack an eye open.

Dad's eyes lock onto me. Here it comes. I cover my head with my arms.

"That performance . . . "

Code Red. Code Red. Run for the forest while I still have the chance. I can live in the trees.

"That was probably the funniest thing I've seen in a while."

I reach out and grab the counter, braced for the grounding of a lifetime.

"I actually laughed all the way home. Mean old Carlotta Watson had that coming."

It takes a second. Finally, I let my arms fall to my

sides. Speckles of ketchup on his jacket look like strange constellations. "You're not mad?"

Dad's shoulders slump forward. "I'm never really mad at you, Dexter. Just concerned. We've been through a lot this year."

I can feel the low hum of the rock through the canvas bag.

Dad's chin trembles. "This is our first Kissmas without her."

I wrap my arms around my dad and hug him tight.

Down the hall, light from the sparkling, pink tree spills out.

Dad hugs me back. "I think I'll drive you and your brother to your grandparents' on Christmas Day."

I pull away, and Dad jams his hands down into his pockets and sighs. "I thought it might be nice for you. They will have a normal tree and decorations, and it will be more fun. We haven't had the time to really do up Kissmas this year."

A hundred million things whiz through my mind at one time, but the biggest one is that we cannot leave Gobbledy alone in the attic, and we cannot take him to G-mama and G-daddy's house, because their house is full of expensive stuff, and there's no attic to hide in.

I shake my head vigorously. "We don't want to do that."

"It's your favorite thing in all the world. That island. The pier. Eating out. Riding around in the golf carts."

Diving in for the save, I tell the truth for the first

time in weeks. "I love my grandparents. I really do. But we can't leave you here alone. This is our home. This is our Kissmas, even if it is without her. We'd like to stay home for the holidays."

Dad puts his hand over his mouth, thinking out loud. "I still have to work."

"Fran is next door," I say, too enthusiastically, but I'm trying to sell him on the idea that I can stay out of trouble, which may not be the case.

Finally, he says, "Really?"

I nod. "Yes, really."

His entire body relaxes, and he lays a hand on the counter. "Well, that's just about the best news I've heard in a while. It's settled. We'll spend the holidays as a family, even if that means acknowledging that we lost one of our own." His expression turns serious. "No going back on this decision when I'm working, and you're bored."

I hold my pinky up in the air. "Pinky swear."

Dad laughs and hooks his pinky in mine. "Okay, but pinky swearing is serious business. I still need to tell your brother. Where is he?"

"In the attic, wrapping presents," I lie.

"Oh, I see."

"I'll tell him. We've already talked about it."

"Well—okay."

A loud chittering sound erupts upstairs. Dad's eyes shoot to the ceiling. "What was that noise?"

The amount of lies I have to tell to get out of this

one conversation is epic, even if it is for a good cause. I have made it this far without going to Code Red. I am not giving up now. "I left the old radio on in the attic. It's probably just static."

Dad's face relaxes again. "Ah, okay. I have to finish a gift out in the garage. We should all stay up late, since there's no work or school tomorrow. I'll make hot chocolate later, like Mom used to do."

I whoop loudly.

Dad smiles. "You know your bag is lit up?"

"What?" I pull the canvas bag off my shoulder and look at it from the side. The corner where the rock is nestled glows faintly. My eyes go wide. "Glow stick," I blurt out.

Behind me, someone knocks on the door so loudly I jump.

Dad steps around me and pulls the door open. I turn to see Fi standing there wide-eyed, with a pinched smile. "Hi, Mr. D.," she says breathlessly. "Did Dexter go to Code Red?"

I shake my head nervously. I'd like to forget the Code Red that didn't happen.

Dad looks confused. "What?"

Inhaling sharply, she changes direction. "Can I talk to Dexter?"

Dad crinkles his face up like she's silly. "Of course." Grabbing a hammer and box of nails off the counter, he says, "I'll be outside if anyone needs me."

"Merry Kissmas," she says quickly, stepping aside to let him pass.

As soon as he's out the door, Fi's mouth drops open, "There is something in the attic you have to see."

Thirty-Six

Gobbledy is waiting for us at the top of the attic stairs. His skinny knees wobble as he bounces up and down.

Dougal hurries around the corner. "How long are you in Code Red?"

I shake my head. "Dad's in the Kissmas spirit."

Dougal cocks his head to the side. "Seriously?"

Fi pushes me up the stairs. "You've really got to see this."

Dougal taps Gobbledy on the shoulder and clears his throat loudly. "Show Dexter."

"Show me what?" I say, cresting the top of the stairs.

Raising an eyebrow, Dougal informs, "While you were downstairs, I asked Gobbledy how he got away from the goons."

Gobbledy runs to the sofa across the room.

I look at Fi, then my little brother, waiting for someone to reveal the big mystery. "Well?" I finally ask.

Dougal maintains eye contact a few seconds longer, then turns to face Gobbledy. "Do you remember what you did when I asked you how you got away?"

Wisps of hair flop on Gobbledy's bent ear as he nods his head.

Dougal walks closer and whispers, "Now, show Dexter."

For a brief second, Gobbledy pulls his fists in tight. Squeezing and squeezing, his whole body trembles. Little sparks of electricity fly from his small body, until *poof*, he disappears.

I'm still watching, but I can't believe my eyes. Fi steps around me into the attic.

Dougal makes eye contact with Fi. "Did you see that on the cameras?"

She pulls her lips tight and nods.

I stumble forward. "What just happened?"

Fi stares at the sofa. "I told you, he's special."

"So, he can disappear?"

Without saying a word, Dougal leads me over to where Gobbledy was standing.

"He disappeared through a hole in the sofa?"

Dougal shakes his head and pokes roughly at the blanket. "See for yourself."

I squeeze my eyes shut, unable to accept the fact that my friend is nothing more than a figment of my imagination.

Clearing his throat, Dougal says, "Open your eyes."

I crack one eye open. On the old blanket, there is a single, golden rock. I step back, reaching for the rock in the canvas bag. It's still inside, warm, with a tiny hum. "Wait. Where did that rock come from?"

Dougal smiles proudly, "That is what you get when you ask simple, direct questions."

"But where did Gobbledy go?"

Dougal carefully picks up the golden rock and holds it in the palm of his hand.

"That's impossible," I say.

"Only to the nonbeliever."

With wonder and hesitation, I touch the rock in his hand. It glows golden and starts to hum.

Fi fills her cheeks with air, then slowly exhales. "These things aren't really rocks. My guess is that Gobbledy can mimic other objects, either because that's the way his species is designed, or because of stress."

"What?"

"He can shapeshift," Dougal says.

I cover my mouth with both hands and mumble, "What does this mean?"

Dougal leans down and whispers to the rock in his hand, "We're going to show Dexter now."

The rock trembles, shudders, and then *poof*, sparks fly. Gobbledy pops back into his normal shape in the palm of Dougal's hand and tumbles onto the sofa, briskly rubbing the fur on his belly.

Outside, swift clouds lift in the dark sky. Moonlight bursts into the attic. The village is suddenly lit with a bright, silver glow. Gobbledy looks so fierce and otherworldly, standing on the edge of the sofa.

Dougal hands Gobbledy a warm juice box and a granola bar. "It's some kind of hibernation. They can change shapes for periods of time, like during travel. It's probably why he likes food so much."

Fi walks around me, over to the sofa. Gobbledy pats the cushion next to him, like he's seen us do.

"I think those mushroom thingies were some kind of electrical source. Something that helped reanimate them," Fi says.

The only girl I know who can use reanimate properly in a sentence.

"He needs a cape," Dougal observes.

Gobbledy snatches the wrapper off the granola bar and chomps loudly, slurping his juice.

The rock warms suddenly in the canvas bag, and hums so low I can hear it. Gobbledy's ears prick up. Within seconds, he has abandoned his juice box, and is climbing up my pant leg.

"What's he doing?"

Fi turns to Dougal and proudly says, "Daddy retrieved the rock."

"What?"

Gobbledy's eyes go wide. I set the canvas bag at my feet and he lets go, falling to the floor. Pawing frantically at the bag, he tilts it to the side, thrusts his arm inside, and pulls out the rock.

If people really have a soundtrack to their life, mine begins right now. Gobbledy holds the rock up, searching for signs of damage.

Dougal reaches for his collection cups. "How did he find them?"

Fi flashes her boldest smile and says, "Daddy has his ways."

When he's finished counting the collection cups, he looks up at me and says, "We're missing two."

Fi holds up a finger. "But we have the rock, and that's the most important part."

The sofa springs groan as Gobbledy bounces up and down, chirping and chattering. Silver light fans out across the room.

"Where is Dad?" Dougal asks.

"In the garage."

"I think it's the electricity," Fi says out of the blue.

"What do you mean?"

"I mean, those mushroom tree things had an electrical current. But, so do our houses. Magnetic fields might reanimate them." She turns to Gobbledy and says, "I want you to tell me where you're from."

Gobbledy chirps in his wild, otherworldly voice, melodic, like a song. Bouncing down to the floor, he presses the rock to his chest, and runs to the telescope.

Mom's telescope. If you angle it perfectly, you can see the sky straight through an opening in the treetops. We're not supposed to touch it. Ever.

Gobbledy clamors up onto the table with the village and pulls the viewfinder to his face.

He clucks at Fi, and she walks over.

Turning knobs and moving the lens all around, he fusses with the telescope until finally, he stops. Stepping aside, he points to the viewfinder, and Fi kneels down, looking.

"Andromeda," she whispers.

Andromeda in my attic. It's the biggest thing to ever happen in my life and it's happening right now.

Fi nods at Gobbledy. "You came a long way, didn't you?"

Wispy hairs on his head fly all around as he nods.

"That's what I thought."

Gobbledy holds his rock out, indicating that he needs something to carry it around in.

Dougal grabs the toy shopping cart and stuffs a blanket inside. He rolls it over to Gobbledy, who climbs down from the table and sets his rock carefully on top.

Fi gives him a good, stern look. "Don't let that rock out of your sight."

Gobbledy chatters loudly and reaches for the handle where he's just tall enough to stretch his long, skinny arms over his head and push the cart.

Fi smiles. "I've got to go. Daddy will be home any second for Christmas. I'll see you guys tomorrow." Pointing at the cameras, she says to Gobbledy, "I've got my eye on you."

Tossing his head back, he chatters like the happiest thing on planet Earth. The most recent transplant, for sure.

"Boys?" Dad yells from the hall.

"Yes, Dad?" Dougal yells back.

"I made hot chocolate like I promised."

Fi grabs her canvas bag and gives Gobbledy a little hug. When she lets go and backs up, he runs and throws his long, skinny arms around her arm.

"Listen," I say to him. "You've got to be quiet for a little while and stay up here."

Gobbledy runs over and pushes his toy cart to the sofa. He climbs on top of the blankets and flops down, feet sticking straight up in the air. With one hand on his rock and the other on his milk bottle, he closes his eyes and within seconds is asleep.

On the way down the stairs, Fi whispers, "What do you think is going to happen with that other rock?"

The very thought gives me shivers. "I'm not sure. I'm just happy I'm not grounded forever."

Fi nudges me in the ribs before running ahead. "Me, too."

In the kitchen, three steaming mugs of hot chocolate are on the counter. Dad wrestles with a bag of marsh-mallows. "Merry Kissmas, Fiona."

"Merry Kissmas, Mr. D.," she says, before running back into the cold.

We all stand in the warm, quiet kitchen. Dougal blows air into his cheeks and then exhales. "We made it."

Dad nods. "We did."

It is true. Through rocks and weird mushrooms, al-most drowning in vats of ketchup, strange new friends, a science project abandoned, and one turned in that's hopefully worth a C, through our first Kissmas without Mom, the moment has arrived, dumping marshmallows into my hot chocolate, with a new friend upstairs.

Dad pulls a tight smile, but I can tell it's genuine. "We're okay. I honestly didn't think that was possible with all the stress I've been under."

Dougal lays a hand on his arm. "We are okay."

I am always amazed by the calming effect my brother has on Dad.

He leans against the counter as I take my first sip of our Kissmas tradition. Warm chocolate and perfectly melted marshmallows remind me that I don't remember when I ate last. My stomach growls in agreement.

Dad laughs, "It sounds like you have a small alien in there," he says, poking my stomach.

I shrug. "If I had an alien, I'd keep him in the attic."

Dougal's smile disappears, and he gives me the stink eye.

Dad stares at me a moment, then laughs.

Dougal glares at me but laughs to play along. This awful *har-har-har* laugh like evil villains in comic book movies.

I drink my hot chocolate and enjoy telling the truth.

The whole truth.

Which hasn't been my thing lately.

Dad suddenly stops laughing and says, "But, seriously, did we forget to eat dinner?" His eyes sweep to the ceiling like he genuinely can't remember.

So, at midnight on the start of our first Kissmas Eve without Mom, I snarf down microwave pancakes and stuff a few in my pocket, just in case someone in the attic catches a whiff.

Thirty-Seven

"Gamma Ray to Cosmic. Come in, Cosmic."

I hear the sound of Fi's voice, but I'm too tired to open my eyes.

Static crackles, then, "Gamma Ray to Cosmic. Come in, Cosmic."

I'm barely awake but pretty sure it's Kissmas Eve and there should be no urgent disasters on holidays. Across the room, Dougal snorts loudly and rolls over, his back to me.

Without opening my eyes, I feel around on the nightstand for my walkie talkie. "Cosmic to Gamma Ray," I yawn.

"Good. You're up," Fi says, in a way that suggests I've been awake for hours, which I haven't. "Look outside," she says urgently.

I open my eyes and stretch before pressing the button to talk. "Front or back?"

"Back," she says, and I can feel her drumming her fingers, waiting.

Dougal is across the room snoring in his rocket ship sleeping bag.

I swing my legs over the side of my bed and look out the window. Down in Fi's driveway, her dad is unloading presents from the back of his SUV. Instead of his usual black suit, he's wearing sweats and a ballcap. One of the boxes is pink with a huge purple bow. Whatever it is, Fi is going to love it. From the looks of it, there are about twenty presents.

I press the button to talk. "That's quite the haul. I'm glad Daddy made it home for Kissmas."

There's a pause, and then static crackles. "*Huh?*"

"You're talking about your dad unloading presents in the driveway, right?"

"Daddy's in the driveway?" Another pause. "Oh, so he is. Huh. Hope that big one is for me. Anyway, that's not what I am talking about. Stand up and look down into *your* backyard."

I push myself up from my bed, and I'm about to ask where to look when suddenly, I know. Right there in our backyard is a treehouse. A real treehouse. Not one of those prefab things, but a real wooden treehouse on the ground, waiting to be put in the huge oak out back.

"Oh. My. God. Fi."

I can see her nodding in my mind. "Yep. You guys got a treehouse."

"Okay. I wanted a dog, but I can live with a treehouse." A big smile tugs the corners of my mouth.

"I can't come over right now because Daddy is about to make us omelets, but sneak up into the attic. Gobbledy has a surprise for you."

I'm not sure how I feel about surprises in the attic.

Dougal rolls over, cracking an eye open, and does not look amused. "A good surprise or a bad surprise?"

Laughter bursts out of the plastic device in my hand. "Go see," she says.

I run quietly because I am certain Dad is still sleeping, but I run, taking the attic steps two at a time, clutching my walkie talkie. I round the corner and slide to a stop. Gobbledy has covered himself and the milk bottle with a blanket. Sleeping with his legs in the air, he has one hand on the golden rock. Everything actually seems to be okay for once.

I know Fi can see me, so I look into the camera mounted in the corner and shrug.

"The village," she whispers.

Turning towards Mom's work table, I see the village is finished. Not perfectly, but there are buildings made of clay, and roads that lead all the way to a set of arches at the edge of the village. There, I see a small clay statue of Mom. She is standing at the entrance, waving good-bye.

Dougal bumps into me from behind. "What's going on?"

I point. His eyes follow my finger and stop on the village.

"Huh," he whispers.

But I know what he's thinking. He's thinking the worst Kissmas has turned into one of the best.

The golden rock hums on the blanket next to Gobbledy.

My walkie talkie crackles to life again. "Okay. I've got a mushroom, double cheese omelet waiting on me downstairs. Daddy's home! He's not here as much as I'd like, but I love it when he is here. Call me when you go out to the treehouse."

"Will do," I say.

Gobbledy cracks one eye open and waves.

Dougal laughs, "He's like a lazy cat."

"But smarter."

"He's going to get us grounded for life."

"Probably."

"Though you have avoided Code Red," Dougal observes.

I pull up straight and tall. "Yes. I did."

I look back over at the statue of Mom waving good-bye. She used to always say, "Life is dirty. Life is messy. Get in there and turn things upside down."

Mom really understood me. Looking at the tiny flowerpots and general store, I realize a few things. The first is, nothing is perfect. Life is life. Perfect is perfect. They don't always meet and greet. Gobbledy and his rocks didn't have a perfect landing, but they're here on the sofa. The few survivors.

The second thing I understand is there is an end. A real end. Even if we don't want it. There is a real end where you have to say good-bye.

That makes me sad. All I did at Mom's funeral was cry. I didn't know what else to do. But now I wonder if Mom's knowledge of the stars helped Gobbledy find us.

Like maybe she was hanging out near Orion's belt and gave his craft a gentle nudge in our direction.

I shrug. Stranger things have happened.

I also learned that people don't go away. They find a place in your heart and stay forever.

Dad's bedroom door opens downstairs and I hear him standing in the hallway, scratching. "Boys? Are you up there?"

I lean over and whisper to Dougal, "Act surprised."

He makes a *pffft* sound and says, "Like I have to *act* these days."

I turn to Gobbledy and whisper, "Stay here. I'll be back in a little while."

Tiny sparks flicker from the golden rock. A gentle hum fills the room. It trembles and shakes and then right before my eyes it goes—*poof!*

Acknowledgments

It takes a lot to write a book. It takes an army of people to bring it to market. A big thanks to Brooke for believing, and to Shannon for all the handholding.

I would like to graciously thank J. Thomas Meador, with whom I have workshopped diligently every week for over a decade. He is an extraordinary writer who makes me bring my best every time. He read every single draft of this novel.

Thanks also to my husband, who is my biggest fan and my greatest love. I love him the way Gobbledy loves food.

The original draft of this novel was written in Peggy Millin's Thursday afternoon writing workshop, where I showed up every week and Alice Johnson cheered me on. To Kelly, and Ginger, and Valerie, and Kimberly, and Peggy, and Maggie: you all inspired me to bring my best to the page. I am grateful for that.

A big thanks to Rachel Stout for giving me about a bajillion notes to make this book shine.

Joy Bagley and her Saturday morning writing workshop changed my life and sent me off on this adventure. She's just about the best writing instructor a girl could ask for.

Maureen Brenner taught me all of what I know

about editing and rewriting and believed in me from the beginning.

Gratitude to Hal and Cheryl, and all they do for writers. Especially this writer :)

A lot of my inspiration comes from influence. For that, I would like to thank Judy Blume, and Peter and Fudge, for creating the marvelous middle grade novel. I read all her books in the early 2000s, and they are awesome. I also owe thanks to Rikki-Tikki-Tavi, the brave mongoose that kept me awake at night; and to Greg & Manny, and Percy Jackson, and Ramona, and Nicodemus, and Wilbur, and Charles Wallace. You entertain and inspire me.

Thanks as well to my grandmother Sara Louise, who would have loved this book.

And lastly, I'd like to thank Peter's turtle.

Especially Peter's turtle.

About the Author

Photo credit A. E. Mueller

LIS ANNA-LANGSTON was raised alongside the winding current of the Mississippi River on a steady diet of dog-eared books. She attended a creative and performing arts school from middle school until graduation and went on to study literature at Webster University. She is a Parents' Choice Gold and a Moonbeam Children's Book Award Winner. She draws badly and sings loudly, and loves ketchup, starry skies, and stories with happy ~~endings~~ aliens. Lis Anna-Langston lives in Columbia, South Carolina. You can learn more about her at www.lisannalangston.com.

SELECTED TITLES FROM SPARKPRESS

SparkPress is an independent boutique publisher delivering high-quality, entertaining, and engaging content that enhances readers' lives, with a special focus on female-driven work.
www.gosparkpress.com

Caley Cross and the Hadeon Drop, J. S. Rosen, $16.95, 978-1-68463-053-0. When thirteen-year-old Caley Cross, an orphan with a dark power, is guided by a jumpsuit-wearing mole into another world—Erinath—she finds a place deeply rooted in nature where the people have animal-like powers and she is a Crown Princess—but she soon learns that the most powerful evil being in *any* world is waiting for her there.

Eye of Zeus: Legends of Olympus Book 1, Alane Adams. $12.95, 978-1-68463-028-8. Finding out she's the daughter of Zeus is not what a foster kid like Phoebe Katz expected to hear from a talking statue of Athena. But when her beloved social worker is kidnapped, Phoebe and her two friends must travel back to ancient Greece and rescue him before she accidentally destroys Olympus.

Inside the Sun: The 8th Island Trilogy, Book 3, A Novel, Alexis Marie Chute. $16.95, 978-1-68463-045-5. All worlds are dying, and it's up to one broken and dysfunctional family to save the day. Each overcoming personal secrets, illness, and trauma, the members of the Wellsley family discover their bravery in the face of all they must face: an enchanted maze, terrifying sea creatures, a fading sun, evil creatures, and a galaxy turned on its head.

The Goddess Twins: A Novel, Yodassa Williams. $16.95, 978-1-68463-032-5. Days before their eighteenth birthday, Arden and Aurora's mother goes missing and they discover they belong to a family of Caribbean deities. Can these goddess twins uncover their evil grandfather's plot in time to save their mother, themselves, and the free world?

The Thorn Queen:A Novel, Elise Holland. $16.95, 978-1-943006-79-3. Twelve-year-old Meylyne longs to impress her brilliant, sorceress mother—but when she accidentally breaks one of Glendoch's First Rules, she accomplishes the opposite of that. Forced to flee, the only way she may return home is with a cure for Glendoch's diseased prince.